CROSSROADS IN TIME

CROSSROADS
IN TIME

PHILBY & ANGLETON
A STORY OF TREACHERY

A NOVEL BY
ANTHONY WELLS

PALMETTO
PUBLISHING

Charleston, SC
www.PalmettoPublishing.com

Crossroads in Time
Copyright © 2022 by Anthony Wells

All rights reserved

Hardcover ISBN: 979-8-88590-034-8
Paperback ISBN: 979-8-88590-035-5
eBook ISBN: 979-8-88590-036-2

DEDICATION

This book is dedicated to two fine and courageous Americans and one much-admired Briton who was "half and half," with an American mother and British father—all of whom were the antithesis of Harold Kim Philby and James Jesus Angleton.

They are Harry Hopkins, President Franklin Roosevelt's highly trusted World War II emissary and adviser; William "Wild Bill" Donovan, war hero and founder and head of the World War II Office of Strategic Services (OSS), the forerunner to the Central Intelligence Agency (CIA), founded in 1947; and Winston Spencer Churchill, wartime leader and prime minister in World War II.

In mid-January 1941, when Britain was in dire straits from the Nazi onslaught, and before Pearl Harbor, Harry Hopkins visited Winston Churchill to reassure him of President Roosevelt's support. At a special dinner in Hopkins's honor in Scotland, Harry Hopkins made a speech at the conclusion of dinner.

He turned and looked at Winston Churchill and said these momentous words:

"I suppose you wish to know what I am going to say to President Roosevelt on my return."

He then quoted from the book of Ruth in the Bible:

"'Whither thou goest, I will go; and where thou lodgest, I will lodge; thy people shall be my people, and thy God my God.'"

Harry Hopkins then paused. He looked again at Prime Minister Churchill and then added in a low, quiet voice, "Even to the end."

Winston Churchill's eyes welled with tears.

These three men exemplify all that is good in American and British culture, and their collective value system and the close bond of their two nations are in huge contrast to the two men you will read about shortly. Human nature is what it is, for better for worse, though one thing is sure: that in the midst of treachery and betrayal, there are always strength, goodness, fortitude, and courage—and those who will always shift the balance back in favor of the right side, an enduring feature of Anglo-American relations and friendship.

CONTENTS

INTRODUCTION

The lives of Harold Adrian Russell "Kim" Philby and James Jesus Angleton intersected almost continuously from their first meeting to Philby's defection to the Soviet Union after being unmasked as a Soviet agent in January 1963. Philby remains to this day the most notorious British traitor, a man whose treachery cost the lives of countless British agents and, by association, those of sister agencies associated with the United Kingdom's Secret Intelligence Service, or MI6. He betrayed a whole generation and more, merciless in his pursuit of obtaining the secrets of British and Five Eyes intelligence—and of their individual and joint relations with third-party foreign-intelligence organizations—and passing these secrets to the Soviet Union via his various handlers.

Philby's relationship with James Jesus Angleton—the chief of counterintelligence at the CIA from 1954 to 1975, with the official title of associate deputy director of operations for counterintelligence—is unique at every level. For the times in which they both lived—Philby died in Moscow on May 11, 1988, aged seventy-six, and Angleton died on May 11, 1987, aged sixty-nine, in Washington, DC—their relationship went far beyond the normal bounds of routine US-UK intelligence liaisons and exchanges. This entailed more than simply performing professional duties for each country in a joint intelligence environment, supported by well-established legal agreements between the United States and the United Kingdom.

It was not just about comparing source material and the resultant analyses and oiling the intelligence machinery of their respective countries. It went beyond these well-established boundaries to a highly personal level of meetings, almost always extremely private, at nefarious nongovernment locations, and clearly very secretive and clandestine, in which there is little doubt that the most sensitive intelligence material was discussed and exchanged. In Washington, DC, they rarely met at either the CIA Headquarters in Langley, Virginia, or at the British embassy on Massachusetts Avenue. This measure was not related to security protocol—avoiding, for example, KGB watchers in Washington, and dodging them by changing locations regularly; rather, they held totally unofficial, nonrecorded, and nonsponsored meetings about which their leadership knew very little, if anything. Their positions of trust allowed them both to pursue this totally unofficial liaison well outside the bounds of traditional tradecraft, since both were senior officials and not undercover agents working clandestinely with false identities. Where else went the critical and highly classified material that they discussed and exchanged is explored in the unfolding plot.

This association and the meetings and interactions that ensued over three decades were unique in the annals of US and British intelligence. No two senior intelligence operatives from the oldest intelligence relationship in the world, between the United States and the United Kingdom, have ever interacted quite like Philby and Angleton. These two bear detailed review, and in light of the benefits of both hindsight and newly obtained material, this novel invites readers to form their own opinions based on the evidence presented as the story unfolds.

This story is in novel format, with a significant element of actual history interspersed between the dialogue and the unfolding plot. This format was chosen not just to make the analysis of the Philby-Angleton relationship more interesting and dramatic—and their lives were certainly all that—but also to invite readers to participate in the unfolding story and to immerse themselves in the intrigue, politics, and massive betrayal of their generation. The alternative of a straight, academic-oriented analysis would not only lose the essence of the life and times of these two complex and utterly despicable men but also perhaps take away the essence of what they were all about, as revealed in both dialogue and the multiple events that show some of the most horrendous betrayals of all time.

There is new material in this novel, never presented and portrayed before. There are certain hypotheses presented, particularly relating to their personal relationship and, perhaps far more important, the culminating events of 1962–1963. The latter involve the drama surrounding the Cuban Missile Crisis and the assassination of President John Fitzgerald Kennedy. The long-term, murky, and totally unofficial dealings of Angleton with Philby reached a zenith, or perhaps nadir is the correct description of their infamous relationship, as the late 1950s and early 1960s unfolded. Angleton's secret visit to Mexico City in the aftermath of a dying CIA chief of station's outstanding attempts to track, report back to Washington about, and thwart Lee Harvey Oswald—who was preparing to reenter the United States from Mexico City, travel to Texas, and murder the president of the United States—is drama in extremis.

This story is chronological, following both main characters from their early beginnings and the foundation of their personalities and inclinations to their activities and relationship until the end of 1963, shortly after the Kennedy assassination, by which time Philby was a Moscow resident. Angleton continued at the CIA until various scandals and investigations into his activities and personal conduct led to him being fired from the agency under the guise of being rewarded with a retirement accolade. In 1954 the director of the CIA, Allen Dulles, had appointed Angleton the head of CIA counterintelligence, a massive error of judgment in retrospect; and on Christmas Eve, 1974, the then director of the CIA, William Colby, demanded Angleton's resignation. Our story ends, therefore, on December 24, 1974, with the ending of Angleton's career. He subsequently died from cancer in May 1987.

There is no evidence that Angleton and Philby connected by any means, either through a surrogate or clandestinely, after Philby's defection to Moscow; and there is no evidence in any of the various interviews in Moscow of Philby by journalists and writers, such as the British author Graham Greene, that Philby discussed his relationship with James Jesus Angleton.

Your author has attempted, and is still working at the time of publication, to find evidence in the KGB and GRU records in Moscow—and in the files of sister services of both entities, post–Cold War Eastern European intelligence allies—of any evidence of operations by the Soviets that connect Angleton back to Moscow after Philby's defection. Angleton assiduously and deliberately either completely wrecked or destabilized the careers of many CIA employees and operatives, several very senior, with false accusations that proved totally unfounded.

One assessment of Angleton's possibly justified counterintelligence paranoia, the Cold War "Reds under the Bed" syndrome, does not hold water in light of the unfolding plot in this story. Angleton, like Philby in his heyday, was thorough and meticulous in the creation of false narratives and totally bogus accusations not just of laudable CIA officers but also of hugely loyal, dedicated, totally secure, and highly competent and well-proven professionals for whom there was absolutely zero evidence of security violations, or worse, working for the other side. James Jesus Angleton, like Harold Kim Philby, was a serious bad actor of enormous proportions, and his positive remembrance in Israel of service to that country is emblematic of his ability to fool even the most prescient of the Mossad. What the Mossad passed to Angleton undoubtedly went to Philby, and we know where it finally ended up: in Moscow.

Please enjoy this story for its revelations, its drama, its record of a past era that may still be with us, though in various new guises, and for lessons to be learned about how two men, with the most evil of intentions, can have a profound effect on the destiny of us all.

Anthony Wells
The Plains, Virginia
December 1, 2021

CHAPTER 1
EARLY BEGINNINGS:
PHILBY AND ANGLETON—THE SCENE IS SET

"The Backs" at Cambridge is enchanting year round and in any weather. It has its own magic that defines the various colleges adjacent to the River Cam and its banks. In the autumn the Backs is particularly attractive, with the trees in their various colors and students punting on the river, enjoying the last of the good weather before winter starts and the various boatyards take up their flotillas of punts.

The afternoon is cloudy, with the sun shining through and the temperature in the midsixties as Kim Philby makes his way back to his college, Trinity, to meet with his friend and fellow student, Guy Burgess. As he ambles along, Philby, full name Harold Adrian Russell "Kim" Philby, reflects on the economics lecture that he has just heard, addressing various aspects of Marxist-Leninist economics versus traditional supply-and-demand capitalist economics characterized by what would become Cambridge's hallmark: "Keynesian economics." Philby's mind is so absorbed in thoughts about Marxism that he almost strays off the footpath onto the bank and the Cam below. He adjusts his stride, as he is running late for his teatime meeting with his fellow student in his Trinity room.

Guy Burgess, full name Guy Francis de Moncy Burgess, is an Eton College graduate who has spent time at Britannia Royal Naval College, also called Dartmouth. He is upper middle class like Philby, and he too is mulling over the notions of capitalist democracy when there is a knock on his college door, and he opens it to find Kim Philby standing there with a ream of college lecture notes grasped in his hands.

"Come on in, Kim," he says. "Tea is on the boil, and I have some excellent crumpets from our favorite bakery."

Philby settles in on the couch in what is one of the better-appointed Trinity rooms, with good, commanding views of the college. As tea is poured, they exchange ideas on their various economics lectures and declare their affinity for the Marxist-Leninist school of thought. Neither is surprised or shocked by the other's views. Both are in their early twenties, both well educated, and both wealthy by any contemporary standards. Burgess asks Philby about his early years in India, where Philby had been born back in 1912 as the Great War was entering a new, dark phase in Europe. Philby excoriates British colonial rule and colonialism in general as an evil capitalist system that is destroying the rights of people like those in India under what he describes as "the British yoke." This is 1934, and Philby is twenty-two. Burgess agrees, and they exchange views on how they would want the world to be and what they think would make it a better place. Both are self-absorbed, and both are physically close, two feet apart, as Philby says two things that will, in retrospect, define not only both their futures but also the lives of countless others around the world—as well as the well-being of the nation that was providing them both with privilege, higher education, and an entrée to the higher ranks of society at large and the upper crust of the British Establishment.

Burgess's hand touches Philby's thigh. It is not the touch of just a good college friend. It is more. Philby does not withdraw. Burgess says in a lone tone, "Kim, I know when there's something on your mind, maybe needling you. Please, get it out. I want to hear whatever it is."

Philby pauses, looks at Burgess, and says in almost affectionate terms, "Guy, you're the best. You know that I don't just admire your views; I'm also very fond of you." Philby then says something that will change the world. "Guy, we are not just birds of a feather intellectually—we are also attracted by several other things that make us a pair."

Burgess's eyes glaze over; he smiles at Philby and listens intently as Kim Philby utters these momentous words.

"Guy, I want you to meet a very good friend, a contact who visits Cambridge to see me from London."

"From your old school, Kim?"

"No," says Philby. "He's from the Soviet Union. He's from Russia, speaks perfect English."

There is a pregnant pause as Burgess sits up and stares at Philby.

"I'm helping him, advising him on my thoughts about Britain, our economy, and why I think our government is all wrong."

Over the next ten minutes, Philby explains in detail about their meetings in various Cambridge pubs and in London, both during term time and the vacations. Philby confesses that he breaks college and university protocols to steal away from Cambridge and buy a daily return ticket to rendezvous with his Russian contact near King's Cross railway station. He adds that the Russian rewards him with generous cash payments that he says, quite unashamedly, enhance his lifestyle. Philby explains that in return he advises his Russian contact about others at Cambridge who may think along Marxist-Leninist lines and who might join this liaison.

There is a pause. Philby looks Burgess straight in the eye and asks very directly, "Would you like to join me in this liaison, Guy?"

A pin could drop. The room is that silent. Burgess returns Philby's look.

"I think that you and I can do great things to make changes for the better," Philby adds.

Philby pauses for only seconds, and Burgess responds, "I'm with you, Kim, whatever it takes. I abhor our system and this government of ours. I'm a committed Marxist."

What happens next is a defining moment.

Both men stand and hug each other. Burgess declares in soft tones, almost a confessional, his sexual preference, and it is not for the ladies. Philby responds in affectionate terms.

The rest of the afternoon, before they break for further study and then formal dinner, with undergraduate gowns worn and the college master and high table dons all present and presiding in the great hall of Trinity, becomes a pattern of behavior.

The man who will become their Russian handler appears on the Cambridge scene in due course, summoned by telephone by Philby, a new recruit in the offing for the Soviet Komitet Gosudarstvennoy Bezopasnosti, better known as the KGB. Both Burgess and Philby will be known by various code names as the years and decades pass. In Philby's case, he will be "Sonny" and "Stanley."

Nineteen thirty-four is a defining year at Cambridge for both men. Their future lives are being transformed and shaped by a distant country about which neither really knows in any kind of detail. The grandiose economic philosophy of *Das Kapital*, also known as *Capital: A Critique of Political Economy*—Karl Marx's defining document written in 1867, with two volumes published later in 1885 and 1894—is an economic treatise that both men study with glee and gratitude to the total exclusion of real-world events. Ironically both Karl Marx and Lenin (who signed in under the name Jacob Richter) have studied in the Reading Room of the British Museum in London.

Neither Burgess nor Philby—nor their other Cambridge KGB recruits who would in due course make up the infamous "Cambridge Five"—knew or indeed understood the full extent of the Stalinist tyranny that was rampant inside the Soviet Union at the time of their recruitment, or the vast number of decent Russians sent to the gulag or disposed of by the Soviet secret police at Stalin's behest. Naivete, combined with high-flying intellectual persuasions, was leading these two men into the paths of betrayal, treachery, and the total abandonment of all that they had been brought up to love, cherish, and admire. Idealism was transformed into a unique brand of sedition, with a self-righteous belief in a cause that they knew only via literature and not real-world experience.

The die was cast. Neither man would ever turn back. They were joined ideologically, intellectually, emotionally, and indeed physically.

In a faraway country, another human being was being molded in a different culture. By late 1934 James Jesus Angleton, born in Boise, Idaho, in December 1917, would be seventeen years old, and he knew little or nothing about a faraway place called Cambridge University, except perhaps as one of the two meccas best known to educated Americans as the doyens of British universities, Oxford and Cambridge. Angleton was intellectually gifted, like his British counterparts, and would in due course go to Yale and Harvard Law School. Before Yale, the young Angleton enjoyed the privilege of attending an English boarding school, Malvern College, for three years, where he became quite enraptured with the culture, way of life, values, wealth, and status of the British Establishment. He never lost his affection and respect for the British way of life—Britons' culture, their mannerisms, and their history. Angleton became steeped in the British lifestyle, traditions, and roles in the world. His first meeting with Kim Philby would be a defining moment in time, with Angleton seeing in Philby all he revered about the educated British upper class. He wanted to be one of them.

At Yale the young Angleton became a serious poet and entered into correspondence with Ezra Pound, T. S. Eliot, and other poetic luminaries while editor of the Yale literary magazine *Furioso*. This was a side of Angleton's character and intellect that is not well known. This was a sensitive side to his personality that would diminish with age, and in some eyes, he would become unbalanced and paranoid. How and why that transformation occurred may explain this major shift not just in his literary sensitivities but also in his view of the world and how he adjusted in his future relationship with Kim Philby.

The Office of Strategic Services (OSS) would be Angleton's entry into the special operations and intelligence world. Little did the OSS founder, Wild Bill Donovan, know, or any of his leadership realize, that they had let into their ranks a Yale graduate with an apparent pedigree yet a disturbed and potentially dangerous personality, hidden views and values, and a distain for those he found stood in the way of his particular modus operandi. Meanwhile, in the United Kingdom, Philby was being invited into Britain's special world by what seemed like the most innocuous route, but beneath the veneer of a Cambridge old boy network lay nothing but deceit, treachery, and betrayal.

CHAPTER 2

THE INVITATION:
A LICENSE FOR BETRAYAL

From Trinity College, Guy Burgess was first well ensconced at the BBC as a producer and then recruited to the British Secret Intelligence Service (MI6), and later to the British Diplomatic Service through the British Foreign Office, with all the privileges and status that these positions conferred. His other identities, "Hicks" and "Mädchen," were known only to his Soviet KGB handlers. Eton, Dartmouth, and Trinity became, as 1939 moved into the disastrous year of 1940 for his country, institutions that he abhorred, and he cleverly worked his way into the heart of British foreign policy. Burgess would become the confidential secretary to Hector McNeil, the deputy to Ernest Bevin, Winston Churchill's foreign secretary. Guy Burgess was dedicated to the Soviet cause, always in his mind rejecting any notion of treason with ill-founded notions of "improving Soviet-West relations." His sexual preferences—developed at Eton and Trinity and during his time as one of the "Apostles" at Cambridge—would now be played out in a new arena. The so-called bankruptcy of the capitalist system would in Burgess's mind be full justification for a move that had disastrous consequences for British security.

Although a member of the British Communist Party, he cleverly disguised his personal and political leanings to further one key objective of his Soviet handlers. He was committed to passing on the most sensitive British secrets to his KGB handlers, and this he did in spades; indeed, he passed on volumes of highly classified documents. His opening came when he could make recommendations for recruitment to MI6, and he recommended those who he knew were already KGB agents. The Soviets wanted him to achieve this as his second primary operational spying objective, in addition to passing on classified material. Kim Philby, on Guy Burgess's recommendation, was about to be inducted into the ranks of MI6, Britain's totally classified agent-running organization.

The pub in Fleet Street was a favorite of Britain's newspaper elite, and that was where Burgess would lay out his plan. Ye Olde Cheshire Cheese at 145 Fleet Street was known for its classic and carefully sourced "pub grub." Rebuilt in 1667, it not only had history, character, and ambience that went with its age—it also had an almost macabre feeling in certain rooms, where generations of newspaper men had discussed, fought over, and then published Britain's latest news.

"Well, Guy," Philby said with an inquisitive smile, "what's up? The Foreign Office crowd treating you well still? And those spooky people over in Waterloo?" Philby was in the newspaper business, a correspondent; he knew the culture, the sources, and the methods of the newspaper business, who knew what and how, and how the best stories were obtained and money made on Fleet Street. He also knew who had and did not have access to government officials, politicians, and people who worked inside the intelligence community. Burgess came to the point quickly.

"Kim, I've got an important opening for you, a great opportunity. One our friends will seriously be pleased with, a chance not to be missed, Kim."

"You've got my full attention, Guy." Philby smirked, with a leer of total anticipation.

"Menzies is on a recruitment drive." Burgess was referring to the head of MI6, Stewart Menzies, a distinguished and highly capable director: "C" for short, named after MI6's first director, Commander Mansfield Cumming, Royal Navy, who always signed documents "C." The title, and eventually the legend, persisted.

"I've been asked to make recommendations. I told Menzies's recruiters from over the way that you, Kim Philby, with all your international travel, journalist contacts, savoir faire, academic credentials, and ease with and access to all the right people—including being a Trinity man, of course—were a perfect choice."

"And so what's happening, Guy?"

"You're a shoo-in. You will fit in perfectly. You'll get a call from one of Menzies's people. The nod and a wink have been given. You're in if that's what you would like. Could lead to all sorts of opportunities. Get you out of this business."

Philby paused, his eyes glazed over. He reached out and touched Burgess's thigh with a deft, almost imperceptible touch. It was the touch not just of a fellow Soviet spy but also of filial affection, indeed, attraction.

"I'm in, Guy," Philby said in a nonchalant and almost malevolent tone. "Time to advance the cause and help Stalin sort out this bloody mess with the Nazis that Chamberlain and his like have created. I hate Halifax and his kind. When do I hear?"

"Soon, very soon. I was asked to approach you and run things by you. That simple. The good old boy network at its best. The British Establishment trusting its finest. Shall I tell them yes, then?" Burgess took a breath and smiled at Philby.

"Absolutely. I'm in, the whole way. Our friends will be delighted. We can find others who are believers too."

"Already on track, Kim," Burgess said in lone tones. "Several of our Cambridge friends will be joining."

The two conspirators finished their pints of English ale.

Burgess then declared, "We'll have key people in all the right places. Our friends will be delighted. I've been passing things on to them, slowly but surely. My copies of state papers, intelligence reports; and I love giving my verbal reports, knowing that they will end up in Moscow, helping our cause, Kim, helping our country by helping those who will stop the Nazi onslaught and create a better world for working people."

Burgess's reference to "our friends" was an oblique recognition of those who were firmly in control of him, Philby, and the others from Cambridge. The KGB had their people in place, on the inside, at the heart of the Foreign Office, MI6, and other key wartime departments.

"Come back to my flat, Kim; I've a special bottle of excellent Bordeaux ready to be cracked open. Come back and enjoy it with me, and we can talk more openly about your new life in 'six.' Time to celebrate, hey?"

Philby almost salivated at the thought.

"Wonderful idea, Guy. You can give me the inside scoop on Menzies's people and what they may have in store for me. What to say and not say, what they may want to hear from me. I need some coaching, please, Guy, a Cambridge-style tutorial on how to convince them I'll make a good spy."

"Spot on, Kim." Burgess leered. "You've got it. I'll tell you how to convince them."

"Let's go," Philby chimed in. "The taxi's on me, and the Bordeaux's on you."

"Perfect," quipped Burgess. He felt that he had made a conquest, a recruit into the inner workings of Britain's Secret Intelligence Service. He had another conquest in mind too. As the taxi slipped away from the Cheshire Cheese, Burgess could not restrain himself. In the rear of the London black cab, Burgess's hand slipped gently onto Philby's thigh.

"You're the best, Kim, the very best. Cambridge's finest. We'll do very well as a team. The six crowd are going to love you."

Philby smiled and looked at Burgess, and his eyes showed one thing and one thing only: intense liking.

Burgess's flat door closed, and the two conspirators headed into the confines of Burgess's very well-appointed flat, one well above the typical income level of his government service grade. Burgess had on his mind other objectives than serving their KGB masters: tasting exquisite and very expensive Bordeaux. Kim Philby was more than his willing MI6 agent-to-be and coconspirator.

The die was cast.

CHAPTER 3

MENZIES'S INNER SANCTUM

Within the inner sanctum of Britain's elite intelligence services, the idea of "positive vetting" had not occurred to anyone as the country faced the Nazi menace, with the fall of France and the daunting prospect of not just an aerial onslaught but also possible invasion. Those who were invited to join the ranks of MI6; the British counterintelligence and security service, better known as MI5; or the much more highly guarded facility at Bletchley Park, north of London, with a totally innocuous title, "the Government Code and Cypher School," were admitted by the most Byzantine and nonsecure means.

It was all about recommendations, who knew who, and who was "the right sort of chap"—someone with a good pedigree, often from an elitist school background, and underneath it all, an old boy network of connections.

Detailed and exhaustive checking into candidates' backgrounds—their detailed personal records, their affiliations, their views on current issues, their financial stability, who they knew socially, where they traveled, and any possible character weaknesses such as alcoholism, and in these years possible vulnerabilities to blackmail and coercion from sexual orientation—did not seem to be a priority. Omitted was the notion that anyone from a solid background with the right pedigree could be anything but loyal, reliable, trustworthy, and most of all, able to keep the nation's secrets closely held. It was trust on steroids: trust in a social hierarchy that was assumed to be infallible in terms of loyalty and integrity. Academic and intellectual achievement, a good school, knowing the right people, maybe sporting success added in for good measure, and personal and confidential recommendations from those "trusted to recommend" were all that was required to breach the inner sanctum of British intelligence.

Kim Philby fit the mold. He had all the appearances of rectitude, sobriety, intellectual attainment, and trustworthiness. Nothing could have been further from the truth.

Stewart Menzies was an unimpeachable director of the British Secret Intelligence Service (SIS), or MI6, from 1939 to 1952. He and Philby could not have been more unalike. He was the antithesis of Philby.

Major General Sir Stewart Menzies had a privileged and wealthy background; he was educated at Eton and fought with great distinction in World War I, receiving a Distinguished Service Order personally from King George V in December 1914. He was honorably discharged from the British Army after suffering from gas attack injuries in 1915. Menzies moved into MI6; by 1929 he was the deputy director to Admiral Hugh Sinclair in the rank of colonel in the British Army, and upon Sinclair's death in 1939 he became director.

Nineteen forty-one is a propitious year for Kim Philby. He meets Stewart Menzies. Philby has to outwit and deceive Menzies when they meet for his interview and convince him that he is the right material for the inner sanctum of British intelligence. Burgess has coached him. He has encouraged Philby to play to Menzies's affinity for the upper class.

Menzies's secretary announces Philby's arrival, and he greets Philby with an amiable handshake and smile that sets the tone for the interview. Coffee is served, and Menzies is easily impressed with Philby's travels as a journalist, his knowledge of Europe, and his successes as an undergraduate at Trinity, Cambridge. The conversation then digresses into more about Philby's pedigree than his potential value as a British agent.

Philby quickly notes that Menzies is more interested in his social background than his skill base and potential usefulness. He is inwardly relieved that he is not questioned on his political beliefs or his commitment to Marxist ideology.

"Guy has given you a very good recommendation, Mr. Philby. I like that. You're the sort of person I need. How well do you know Spain and the

Spanish? Franco is no friend to us. He's in bed with Hitler and the whole Nazi apparatus that supported him during the Spanish Civil War."

Philby pauses and cleverly plays to what he thinks Menzies wants to hear.

"My journalist days taught me a lot about Spain, the Spanish, and how Franco operates. I think that I could help a lot in undermining Spanish influence on Salazar, for example."

"Excellent, excellent," Menzies repeats, "I need a good man to take charge of our Iberian section, which needs a strong hand. Our agent base in Gibraltar and across the strait in Tangier is weak; we need to guard the western Mediterranean and prepare for whatever Hitler has in store for Portugal and monitor Salazar's relationship with Hitler."

"Yes, indeed, sir," Philby responds, sitting up straight and looking Menzies dead in the eye. "I'm very familiar with our dependence on Portuguese iron ore and tungsten, just as Hitler's war machine is. We need to protect our interests."

"I may offer you the lead job in our Iberian section. Would that interest you? You seem ideally suited for what I need."

Philby realizes that he has passed the test; he's being offered an actual position, and he responds accordingly.

"Sir, I would be honored to head up that section. I think that I can do just what you need to expand our agent base and grow our intelligence."

"Splendid, Philby, splendid," responds Menzies. We'll get the necessary paperwork to you soonest, and I would like you to start as soon as possible. Is that doable?"

"Most certainly," Philby replies. "I am freelancing, so I'm very flexible."

"Perfect cover—no one will know you've moved into our world. I like that."

They chat about who Philby knows and discuss his Cambridge friends, and Menzies makes a direct comment about how pleased he is that Guy Burgess had brought Philby to his attention.

A second cup of coffee is enjoyed over further pleasantries and discussion of Philby's London location and easy ability to join MI6 in Menzies's headquarters building.

Menzies presses his buzzer, and his secretary enters.

"Mr. Philby is joining us. Prepare all the usual paperwork, please, and have him sign the Official Secrets Act before he leaves."

Philby politely inquires about a joining date.

"Soonest, absolutely soonest—give us until next week, if you can wrap things up on Fleet Street."

"Yes, indeed, sir, I can be here a week on Monday, if that works."

"Excellent. I'll make arrangements to have you fully briefed and read into all our Iberian operations by my deputy."

"Thank you, sir. I am looking forward to working hard and doing what I hope will be an outstanding job for you."

"Thank you, Kim."

Menzies shakes Philby's hand and with a wry smile says, "Welcome to the club. You fit perfectly."

Menzies's secretary escorts Philby to the exit and wishes him a good day.

Philby notices that Menzies and his secretary seem to have a special rapport, almost personal as much as professional. It is about how they look at each other.

Philby has made a subtle observation.

He hails a taxi and heads back to Fleet Street.

On returning to Menzies's office, his secretary closes the door, and a very personal conversation takes place about Philby. Menzies asks her what she thinks about him. She says that she likes him and that he would fit in well.

Menzies steps across from his desk; the door is closed, and he embraces his secretary with a passionate kiss that is reciprocated in like manner. Menzies and his secretary have more than just a professional relationship.

Meanwhile Philby is almost salivating as his cab heads over Waterloo Bridge, turns down the Strand, and heads for Fleet Street.

He plans to see Burgess in his flat that evening and celebrate in more ways than one.

The inner sanctum has been breached. The KBG will shortly have its man in place in the very heart of the British Secret Intelligence Service.

CHAPTER 4

BIRDS OF A FEATHER FLOCK TOGETHER

Angleton slid into the brainchild of William "Wild Bill" Donovan, the Office of Strategic Services (OSS), like a hand inside a silk glove. He had joined the US Army in 1943 and soon found himself a natural selectee for the fledgling OSS—well educated, with an international background by American standards of the day, and assumed to be trustworthy given his family background, upbringing, and Yale and Harvard Law School antecedents. He was in a key position of trust from the word *go*. He moved up quickly and soon found himself leading the OSS branch in Italy, eventually ending up in Rome after its liberation from the Nazis and the fascist government of Benito Mussolini.

Norman Holmes Pearson of the OSS selected Angleton to join him in London to head OSS's counterintelligence branch (X-2), making him the chief of the Italy desk in February 1944; and later that year, in November, Angleton moved back to Italy as commander of OSS's Secret Counterintelligence Unit (SCI) Z.

While he was in London, things happened that shaped the future in ways that few could ever have predicted.

Norman Holmes Pearson not only trusted Angleton implicitly, he also regarded him as one of his finest.

"James, the folks over in six want to meet with you, and I've arranged with Stewart Menzies for you to go over to their place and get introduced and briefed into what SIS is up to in Italy."

Angleton was overjoyed. He was going to be indoctrinated into the British Secret Intelligence Service's innermost secrets about Italy and at the same time become introduced to the Bletchley Park Enigma intercepts of Nazi-Italian machinations and what Hitler's staff was planning after Mussolini's collapse.

"Sir, I look forward to meeting with C's people. I've heard a lot about how Director Menzies runs a pretty sharp organization."

"You bet you do," quipped Pearson. "They're the best, together with the Room 39 crowd that run British naval intelligence. It was the navy people, led by Vice Admiral John Godfrey and his brilliant assistant, Ian Fleming, who inspired Wild Bill to set up our show. OSS owes a lot to the Brits and their NID. Their navy people have been running Bletchley hand in glove with our ONI in Washington and out in Pearl Harbor."

"Who's my point of contact at six, sir?"

Pearson paused for a moment.

"I'm wondering if they have someone who knows Italy as well as I do," Angleton said.

"Yes, Menzies gave me a name. A guy called Philby, Kim Philby, Cambridge man, supposed to be pretty smart, and he has been involved in their SOE as well as running ops in the Iberian Peninsula. I'm not sure how well he knows Italy and the contacts you have in Rome."

Pearson was referring to Winston Churchill's creation, the Special Operations Executive, SOE for short, that he created to "set Europe alight."

"They'll brief you on what they're up to, and I gather Philby has his fingers in lots of pies, so he may be a good contact for other things besides Italy."

"Thank you, sir. I'll get going, read the background briefing that your staff has given me, and head on over for the appointment."

"Good luck, keep me posted, and let me have a report on what you learn and what we need to do to help our British friends, and of course vice versa."

"Will do, sir."

Angleton returned to his office to find a message—to call Kim Philby.

Philby answered the phone when Angleton called.

"Philby here. Oh yes, James Jesus Angleton, great American names, only in America. Look forward to meeting. I think your boss will have filled you in on a little bit about our various goodies over here."

Before Angleton could say much more than a short "hello" and "look forward to meeting," Philby shot one across Angleton's bow.

"Look, let's meet off site, somewhere discreet—a private café where we can talk without all the chatter going on in the office here."

"Whatever you suggest," Angleton replied. "Do you have a place in mind?"

"Let me introduce you, James, to one of the finest cups of tea that you can find in London."

"I'm all ears, Kim, but bear in mind that I was weaned for a few years on good old British tea while at school over here."

"Malvern College, I believe, James. Read it in your file."

"Well, well, you do know something about me then."

"Your boss sent over a short bio to my director."

"So where are we gathering?"

"Twinings, old boy, the oldest and finest tearooms in London. Founded by a chap called Thomas Twining back in the early seventeen hundreds, if my memory serves me correctly. I think their founder created Earl Grey tea."

"Impressive. I cannot wait for—how do you Brits say it? My first 'cuppa' of Twinings. So where do I head?"

"Two one six the Strand. Short cab ride for you, James."

"What time, please?"

"Three this afternoon, for traditional English afternoon tea. My pleasure."

"Thank you. I may arrive a tad earlier just to explore. Sounds like a piece of hidden British history."

"Absolutely, James. See you later today. Goodbye."

Philby put the phone down in his MI6 office, sat back, and breathed deeply. His mind raced. He knew more about Angleton than he had implied. His personal life was an open book—intriguing, in fact. Where did this smart and well-educated American stand in the great scheme of things? A poet at one level of intellectual activity, yet at another he was clearly dedicated to the defeat of the most insidious regime in history, Hitler's Nazis. Where did he stand regarding Stalin and the Soviet Union? Had he shown proclivities toward a left-wing world after the war?

Philby mused further about his tearoom guest's possible weaknesses and how he might induce him into joining the cause. At the same time, Philby hesitated in his mental gymnastics about recruiting Angleton to consider possible counterintelligence by the Americans. Angleton had evidently done a very commendable job in Italy in tracking down the undercover fascist and Nazi sympathizers who had given succor to Hitler's and Mussolini's worst activities. In a mental flash, Philby recalled the Americans' countercommunism plans for a postfascist Italy. Was Angleton part of the American efforts to stamp out Moscow's growing influence to impose communism in a postwar Italy?

Philby knew one thing. He had to tread carefully. Central to his strategy would be benign neutrality on current issues and letting Angleton do the talking. Listening would be the name of the game. As Philby closed his Italian file, he wondered if Angleton had personal weaknesses, hidden from his American colleagues and records. Time would tell. Meanwhile Philby planned to exchange tradecraft and secrets and establish a level of confidence for future exploitation of any weaknesses that he might detect in Angleton's personal profile.

Philby had determined above all else one key aspect of what he hoped and planned to be a burgeoning relationship, namely to obtain American secrets that the British did not have and pass them on to his KGB controllers. Somewhere, Philby surmised in his evil machinations that there might be a way into Angleton's mindset that would permit him to be the unwitting handmaiden of Soviet intelligence. Philby might be able to play on his inner being, to exploit perhaps an overbearing desire to be the best of the best in American counterintelligence, and to get him to tell all, even if he remained a stalwart of American decency and loyalty.

Philby had a plan. At one level it was ingenious and artful in extremis; at another it was simply thoroughly evil and threatened the very heart and soul of the special relationship that had flourished since Winston Churchill and Franklin Roosevelt met on board the HMS *Prince of Wales* in Placentia Bay, off Newfoundland, on August 10, 1941. This meeting occurred several months before Pearl Harbor, while many in the United States, in Congress, in the media, and in the public at large were still against any American intervention in the European war. Churchill and Roosevelt, together with their key military staffs, created in the utmost secrecy, unbeknownst to the British and American people, a grand strategy for the defeat of Hitler and the creation of the Atlantic Alliance.

Philby was in the business of supporting Stalin and the communist regime in the Soviet Union, an ally after the Nazi invasion of the Soviet Union, Operation Barbarossa, began on June 22, 1941. This invasion broke the nonaggression pact that Germany and the Soviet Union had signed two years earlier. The largest German military operation of World War II augured the defeat of Hitler's Wehrmacht, culminating in its defeat in the momentous Battle of Stalingrad.

Philby felt exhilarated and profoundly uplifted by his chimerical dreams of a postwar communist world. Meanwhile he must serve his Moscow masters, and this would require skillful treachery, seductive entrapment of the willing and naive, and in the case of Angleton, moving gradually so that the American would not perceive the sinister and pernicious nature of Philby's intent.

Philby's game plan evolved, and he planned each step in his sinister plot to exploit his American guest at afternoon tea.

CHAPTER 5
TEA AND MORE THAN SYMPATHY

Twinings's wonderful tearooms and shop more than lived up to Angleton's expectations. He arrived early—a good fifteen minutes before Philby timed his entrance. He loved the history and the fact that he would indulge in the world's finest tea in a building that still had the aura of its founder, Thomas Twining.

Angleton did some simple math. The teahouse had been founded in 1706—it was still in the same building, serving exquisite teas, in fact—and built seventy years before the American Revolution. He was inspired, and as he walked around the tearooms of all tearooms, the poet in him created a few lines about soothing teas and fine thoughts. Angleton reflected that Paris might have its Les Deux Magots in Saint-Germain-des-Prés, where Hemingway, Simone de Beauvoir, Jean-Paul Sartre, Albert Camus, Pablo Picasso, James Joyce, and others gathered to drink and intellectualize, but this center of tea bliss was more than just special. It was very private, reserved—indeed, soothing. Little did he realize that his host had other intentions for him. He would be shown old-fashioned British manners and largesse, kind treatment and care for an American in a London at war, lots of tea, and sympathy, but also the cunning manipulation of a crucial ally.

The waiter seated them at Philby's request in a quiet and discreet part of the tearooms, with no eavesdroppers nearby to overhear their conversation. Their first meeting was to be one of many over the coming years. The American handshake, the British largesse, the table manners, and the fine teas all combined to quickly lure Angleton into a sense of security and trust.

Philby was at his British best. He asked after Angleton's personal situation in London and offered help with accommodations and willingness to invite him to social gatherings where he could meet and mix with the "right kind of people," who would provide Angleton with fine company, good food and wine in spite of the rationing, and insight into British politics. After Angleton responded with sincere and somewhat platitudinous comments about the crucial value of the US-UK alliance, Philby complimented Angleton on his Italian successes and subtly supported the United States' anticommunist policy for Italy while cleverly leaving the door open for an alternate view of Italy's future. Within ten minutes Philby had set the stage for a deeper set of subjects.

Angleton was the first to extend the normal boundaries in a tearoom.

"Kim, I have to tell you that without your people out at Bletchley and Masterman's extraordinary team, we would all be in deep trouble. We're indebted to British ingenuity—indeed, genius is how our technical people describe what some of your best and brightest have achieved. Simply amazing."

"Spot on, James. We recruited the right people from the right places in the nick of time. Close-run thing, to quote the Duke of Wellington after Waterloo. We managed to get things set up before the Nazis struck."

"Imagine life without Enigma and Double Cross," said Angleton in a very low voice, almost so low as to be inaudible.

Philby picked up on it.

"Sharing all that data is what it's about, an alliance built on trust and mutual respect. We need to go several steps further to ensure that we stay on top and don't let the Hun know what we have—pure gold."

"Couldn't agree more, Kim. What I'd like to do is build on these foundations and go onwards and upwards until we beat the lot of them. OSS has several ideas that we want to share with you. My own strength and personal domain is counterintelligence, watching out for the bad guys in our midst and also in places like Italy and other parts of Europe, once liberated. I'd like to work with you if we can, explore how US and British counterintelligence can ferret out those we shouldn't trust both now and in the years to come, hopefully when we've beaten the Nazis and the Japanese."

Philby machinated and changed tack. He realized that Angleton was opening the door. He did not have to ask. It was being offered.

Over the next hour, both men, heads bowed, tasting Twinings's finest and eating their exquisite delicacies and cakes, explored multiple ways ahead and options—not just for undermining the Nazis but also for a vision of the postwar world and how they could both contribute, together. Philby realized, without showing one shred of disagreement, that he was building a relationship not just on firm intelligence-sharing foundations but also on a private, indeed very private, and secret personal understanding. This was between two men, not two countries and allies.

The future chief of CIA counterintelligence from 1954 to 1975 was now in an exquisite tearoom in London in the middle of World War II, offering Kim Philby an open door to US intelligence. This was personal. This was not government to government. This was about a relationship. They liked each other. They were drawn together by each other's kindred personalities, cultured ways, sense of superiority, intellectual arrogance, and, underneath it all, a simple, positive attraction. They were made for one another at one level, beyond the professional relationship, beyond the mutual sense of superiority, on another plane of interpersonal self-aggrandizement. They loved what they exchanged.

Philby was adroit at not giving even a glimmer of his Marxist-Leninist ideology to Angleton, a fatal step if taken. He praised American capitalism as the savior of the Western world and the democracies—"A beacon," as he called it, "for the millions who have suffered under Nazism." He failed, of course, to recognize the worst of Stalinism and its appalling record of the suppression of the opponents and rivals of a man who symbolized the gulag in all its horrific brutality.

The parting of the ways from the esteemed teahouse culminated in a firm and unequivocal understanding that they would continue to meet privately, share information, and discreetly yet quasi-officially agree on tactics, techniques, and procedures for their respective organizations to stay on top, defeat the Nazis, and build a better world.

As they stepped out onto the Strand, there was a certain headiness in their farewell as they hailed black cabs, smiles and eyes that revealed unmistakable liking. Their parting was just the beginning of a relationship with momentous consequences.

Treachery would know no bounds.

CHAPTER 6
CONSOLIDATION WITHOUT COMPROMISE

Angleton would go to work for successive American intelligence luminaries: General Walter Bedell Smith; Allen W. Dulles, brother of the US secretary of state John Foster Dulles; Richard Helms; and William Colby—all directors of the CIA after its formation in 1947. What he and Philby did together before 1947 set the stage for Angleton's CIA career. The creation of the fledgling CIA coincided with Philby's appointment to Washington, DC, to be the critical MI6 liaison officer in the British embassy. The World War II personal liaisons and private meetings persisted throughout Philby's time in Washington, with intimate exchanges and intelligence passed in the most unofficial of ways. At the same time, Guy Burgess was also in Washington, DC, on the staff of the British embassy, and lived in Philby's Washington home.

At the personal level, Angleton married a Vassar College alumna, Cicely Harriet D'Autremont, in July 1943—not unusual at his age in the middle of a war. There is little known about this relationship and Angleton's other female relationships. However, his relationship at the professional and personal level blossomed with Philby, from their first meeting to when Philby was expelled and recalled from Washington after Guy Burgess and Donald Maclean defected to Moscow in 1951. The Venona project intercepts had exposed both these British spies, two of the Cambridge Five. Philby was suspected by association, was investigated and found not to be implicated, and disappeared into the journalist world until later evidence showed that he was indeed the arch-Soviet agent.

In spite of Angleton's very close association with the discredited Philby, the director of the CIA in 1954, Allen Dulles, appointed Angleton head of counterintelligence. On Christmas Eve 1974, Director Colby demanded Angleton's resignation. Angleton had survived a long and dangerous path with untold damage done, even after Philby's defection to the Soviet Union. How could this be?

The Old Ebbitt Grill is the oldest restaurant in Washington, DC, and has cachet all its own. This was one of Angleton's favorite restaurants and one of three locations where he liked to have his several-hours-long tête-à-têtes with Philby. They would typically meet at noon and often not depart until 3:00 p.m., and sometimes even later if the maître d' plied them with several of their favorite cocktails. Neither would return afterward to his respective office at Langley or the British embassy. Neither reported in writing the substance of their meetings nor gave detailed verbal reports.

Philby would occasionally mention to his staff within the confines of the MI6 liaison cell at the embassy that he would be out of the office meeting with his CIA contact, and similarly with Angleton—he would keep his personal secretary aware of his movements. His reports back to the director of operations at the CIA, the official head of the clandestine HUMINT arm of the agency, were never kept in the loop.

Philby had often entertained Angleton at the Ritz, on Piccadilly, in London, for lunch and often for their scrumptious afternoon high tea. The Old Ebbitt Grill had its own unique aura, and it was here that some of the most sensitive of American and British secrets exchanged hands and ended up in the heart of KGB headquarters in Moscow.

"Welcome, first secretary," is Angleton's initial salutation to Philby. It is September 1949, and both men are on career rolls. Angleton is a heavy drinker and loves his martinis. Philby participates while clearly keeping his mind clear to steer Angleton into the most sensitive domains.

"How's the embassy, Kim? The ambassador still treating you well, I trust?"

"Same old, same old, James. Let's order. I'm starving. I had nothing for breakfast. Saving myself for the Ebbitt's finest." They order the first two courses after downing their initial martinis—vodka for Angleton and gin for Philby.

"Oliver Franks is a good man, James, the best that Britain could send over here. Certainly a damn sight better than Halifax, Chamberlain's man. Winston did the British and the world a service by sending him to Washington. Got him out of the way, thank God, and let Anthony Eden run the show. I like Oliver, get on well with him, and he lets me do my own thing. Being a good Foreign Office man, he knows how to stay clear of six and what we get up to, but he likes to get caught up to date on how our liaison with you guys is progressing, so I keep him well informed, maybe once every couple of weeks."

"Does he see your reports?"

"No, not unless there's something urgent that you and I know about and he needs to know before I contact C."

Philby is referring to the director of MI6, who was always known as C, after the very first director, Commander Mansfield Cumming, Royal Navy, who was in the Secret Intelligence Service 1909–1923. Cumming always signed himself on papers as "C," and the tradition persisted.

"Oliver is outstanding. Knows how to balance things and does not micromanage. Trusts us to do our jobs."

"Good, that's really good, Kim. Well, I've got some serious news for you, Kim, in addition to some follow-up gems from my friends in Israel. God, do they love me in the Mossad. Hope it never changes. Absolute gems coming out of the Soviet Union through all those émigrés and Jewish refugees."

"Tell me more," says Philby.

"Nuclear things. After the Reds detonated their first bomb in forty-nine, they've been feeding me gold about how they're reacting to our moves over here. I'm getting A1 material from several Israeli sources, highly reliable. All technical stuff, and who's driving the Soviet bomb train. I owe them big time."

"What's the quid pro quo, James?"

Angleton pauses. His eyes become steely.

"They'll want help themselves eventually."

"With what?"

"A nuclear weapon, of course," Angleton says in the lowest of tones.

"Take a look at this." He opens the *Washington Post*, and hidden in the middle are several pages of Mossad reports.

Angleton hands the newspaper to Philby.

"Read it, Kim. It's the best. I can't give you a copy. Instead I've hand-written a summary—a bunch of notes you'll see at the end. Yours. Keep them close. Your eyes only."

Philby looks up at Angleton.

"You're the best, James. I'll return the favor. I have a way."

Angleton is intrigued and awaits Philby's offer.

"You know, James, I learned a lot when I worked for SOE during the war."

Philby is referring to his time at Brickendonbury Estate in Hertfordshire, England, where Philby, very inexperienced himself, ran an SOE course. Later he was a trainer at another SOE facility, Lord Montagu's estate in Beaulieu in Hampshire, England. By September 1941, with little under his belt except his journalism experiences, Philby became head of MI6's Iberian section, covering Spain and Portugal.

Philby knows how to play Angleton like a violin.

"James, I've access to all the nuclear technology data."

"How come?" inquires Angleton. "I get all my stuff from the Israelis. Our nuclear people don't share a thing with the agency."

"Well, I have way round all that for you, James."

"Tell me more."

"We've a top British nuclear scientist at the embassy. Wilfrid Mann is his name. He has access to everything. He's our link between the US programs and our people back in the UK, the very top scientists, Teller's and Oppenheimer's equivalents."

"And so how do you fit in? Do they give you access?"

"Not quite, James."

"Well?"

"Mann brings all the material to me to transmit it back to the UK on my cipher machine. He leaves it with me. I have a present for you, James."

Angleton is little aghast, though elated. He can hardly believe what Philby is doing, and furthermore, Philby reaches down to his attaché case and lifts out a manila envelope.

"From MI6 with all my many thanks for our great relationship, James."

Philby hands him US-UK highly classified nuclear secrets.

"It's a copy, James. Mann leaves the material with me. This is a copy for you of all the key material we've been sending to the UK recently."

Angleton beams.

"Thank you, Kim. This is the special relationship at its best." He beckons the waiter and orders two more martinis.

"I've something special for you, too, Kim. It will have to wait. I'm working a very sensitive subject right now. I'm waiting for more details. Once I have them, I'll share. You'll be impressed."

"Well, that's a very nice quid pro quo, James. I'll be patient."

"Kim, my Israeli contacts are the best. You'll love them. If you go back to the Middle East, I'll hitch you up with them. I have access to the top of the Mossad."

The two men eat their expensive lunches and wallow in their own vanities and conceits, totally unknowing of each other's hidden agendas and loyalties.

Little does Angleton know at this point that Philby is soon to have living in his Washington home a man who is joining the British embassy in Washington. This person is none other than Guy Burgess.

Philby and Angleton part company. It is almost 4:00 p.m. This has been a megalunch, gratis the CIA. The CIA picks up the tab, drinks included.

The American taxpayer will know nothing of these expenditures. Angleton and Philby live in secret worlds in which expense accounts are classified and audits unheard of except to be a basis for further funding of so-called clandestine activities.

Philby watches as Angleton's cab takes him homeward.

Philby has another rendezvous planned.

After several circuitous and hugely cautious route changes, Philby arrives at a small park near Rockville Pike.

Philby's KGB contact and handler has executed even more complex evasion techniques in case the counterintelligence arm of the Federal Bureau of Investigation (FBI) is on to him.

The Soviet operative does not ever go near the Soviet embassy. He is deeply buried under the guise of a Soviet import-export executive, buying quality American beef and importing Russian vodka and the like.

Philby triple-checks the area, as does the KGB man.

They are like ships passing in the night.

Philby leaves his newspaper on the park bench with the same US-UK nuclear material that he only one hour before had handed to Angleton.

The KGB man leaves his copy of the *Washington Post* at another location nearby, on a park bench where he has been sitting, reading.

Within are instructions in code about the next meeting, where and when. These are simple and are adjacent to the crossword puzzle. All very innocent.

Philby then proceeds out of the park and checks and double-checks for surveillance.

As he leaves, he sidesteps to a trash container at the side of the path, drops a small piece of trash, and discretely recovers a small envelope taped to the inside of the container.

Later he will open and retrieve his ill-gotten gains: several thousand US dollars.

Angleton arrives back at his home, elated with a great day's work with his prize MI6 contact.

CHAPTER 7

THE OCCIDENTAL GRILL AND TABARD INN: SPY AND FOOD CONNOISSEURS

The Occidental Grill and the Tabard Inn were two of Angleton's other favorite locations for his rendezvous with Philby. They were perhaps not in the same league as the Old Ebbitt Grill in Angleton's scheme of things, but they were plenty good enough for fine food and drinks while the two men exchanged their nations' most treasured secrets. Angleton was becoming a heavy drinker and eater. Philby helped him indulge his tastes. The more he was plied with hugely expensive wines and fine cocktails, the more Angleton would sing for his lunch—and often his supper too.

Philby leaves his house on what would be a propitious and earth-shaking day, accompanied by Guy Burgess. Philby drives. Burgess has a serious hangover as a result of major overindulgence the night before. Burgess is bleary eyed and slightly incoherent as Philby explains, as they drive along Massachusetts Avenue, his game plan for the day: a discreet meeting planned with Angleton at the Occidental Grill. Before he departs the embassy for the Occidental Grill, Philby explains that he, the "first secretary," will have a special MI6 gathering in his office to plan out the next few weeks, followed by a scheduled thirty-minute update one on one with the British ambassador.

Philby rarely chastises Burgess for his drinking habits. This morning he is worried more from an embassy perspective. Will Burgess's diplomatic masters pick up on his continued waywardness? Philby is worried, along with their KGB handlers, that Burgess's habits are becoming too public, too obvious not to be noticed by the senior Foreign Office staff. Philby has been tipped off by his secretary that "Mr. Burgess seems to like one too many."

"Guy, we're as close as it gets." As he drives, Philby is telling Burgess that he cares about him in more ways than one.

"Your living with me is good for many reasons, Guy. We both know that. It's wonderfully good for our special connection—not just us, but also for our relationships with you-know-who."

He pauses as he encounters the morning Washington traffic.

"What are you trying to say, Kim?"

"Simple. We have to be careful, very careful. People are talking about you—yes, you, Guy, and it's your taste for the bottle that's garnering attention."

"OK, I understand, and so?"

"Well, please just be much more discreet in the embassy and at all the social events. Don't indulge too much, please. The deputy's a tough character; I can protect you with the ambassador, but his number two is a different kettle of fish, and he rules the roost when it comes to staff matters and who stays and who goes."

"Am I in danger? Is that what you're saying?"

"No, just be a lot more careful, more discreet. Don't give grounds for suspicion, for God's sake. My biggest fear is our security people having the FBI check you out. Our people are pretty lackadaisical and ineffective, but if the FBI were called in to keep an eye on you, that's another matter altogether."

"I see. I'll be careful, Kim. I promise."

As they enter the embassy, the guard lets Philby's car through with a smile and salute. He parks in his own spot, and before Burgess alights, Philby looks at him.

"Guy, you know how I feel about you: please, please be careful. We may be treading on thin ice."

"Got it, Kim, say no more. I'll shape up, I promise you."

As they leave the parking area, Philby notices that Burgess's gait is less than straight and he is slouching along.

"Come on, Guy, walk tall; people are watching."

They enter the British embassy, and the day begins. At this point, little does Philby realize that his words with Burgess are not just prophetic but profoundly accurate.

After the MI6 staff meeting and the short thirty-minute briefing with the ambassador, Philby spends time checking all his message traffic from MI6 headquarters. Nothing gets his immediate attention, and he feels comfortable in meeting his luncheon appointment with James Angleton.

"Mr. Angleton called to confirm, sir," Philby's secretary says. "He looks forward to seeing you at eleven thirty at the Occidental Grill. I have checked with their reservations people, sir. You're all set for your usual table."

"Thank you. I may be out until midafternoon. I may go back to Langley with Mr. Angleton. If I'm not back by four, don't expect me. I'll see you in the morning."

"Very good, sir." She then adds in a low tone, "I checked with their security people. You're good over at Langley indefinitely. No need for our people to keep passing your clearances."

"Excellent. Thank you," replies Philby. "The Americans owe us, big time, and fortunately people like James Angleton understand all that. Our special relationship is very special. None of us want to rock the boat. The prime minister and president are absolutely solid when it comes to intelligence exchange."

His secretary nods in total agreement with her boss's words. "Yes, sir. You make it all happen."

It is fall in Washington, DC, as Philby drives to meet Angleton. Philby looks back on World War II, his first ever meeting with Angleton, and all that has transpired since. Now he is driving to meet privately with the man who provides him with sheer gold for his Soviet masters. He thinks about how his KGB handlers paid him handsomely for his revelations to them, and therefore to Stalin himself, about Hitler's plans to invade the Soviet Union in Operation Barbarossa, as well as British intercepts that indicated that the Japanese were intending to strike in Southeast Asia. He has forever endeared himself to the KGB.

With the material that Maclean passed on to his KGB handlers from the Joint Intelligence Committee in London, Philby, together with Burgess, was providing their Soviet masters with the greatest of US and UK secrets. However, little did Philby know that the JIC did not have access to the American Manhattan Project atomic bomb information or British nuclear secrets. Donald Maclean had no knowledge of these and could not pass on critical nuclear plans and technology. Philby had obviated all this to a certain extent by passing on the material that went through his cipher machine from Wilfrid Mann and from the Israeli Mossad's sources and methods.

Maclean's and Burgess's webs were about to be untangled in the most secretive of ways. Little did the Cambridge Three of Philby, Burgess, and Maclean realize that there were others in the game besides themselves and their Soviet puppet masters. If Burgess and Maclean were "two," then Philby was indeed "the third man." The 1949 film of the same name, directed by Carol Reed—from the book by Graham Greene and starring Orson Welles, Joseph Cotton, Alida Valli, Trevor Howard, and Bernard Lee—marked the beginning of the end of not just the third man but also his two notorious accomplices and fellow Soviet agents.

James Jesus Angleton had no idea or sense of history or destiny as he departed Langley and drove down the George Washington Memorial Parkway toward his rendezvous with Harold Kim Philby. As the CIA headquarters' guards saluted him and he joined the midmorning traffic, all that Angleton could think about was the highly classified material that he would now disclose to Philby.

CHAPTER 8
DENOUEMENT: VENONA SPEAKS

Philby did not have regular access during World War II to all the Bletchley Park Enigma intercept material. He saw certain things, or was briefed on them, but fortunately never had total access.

Angleton was about to change one key dimension of all this as Philby parked his car at the Occidental Grill. As he locked his car door, he took a deep breath. Angleton had called him the previous evening to say that he had important news for him. It was critical that Philby keep their luncheon appointment.

At 11:30 the restaurant was still mostly empty. Philby was ahead of Angleton, who had been delayed back at CIA headquarters by what he would now reveal to Philby. Philby waited patiently, scanning the menu and wine list multiple times.

Angleton was running late as he left the George Washington Memorial Parkway and turned right at the exit that led up to Key Bridge and across the Potomac River. As he drove into the District of Columbia, Angleton reflected on his relationship with Philby: much more than just two senior intelligence officers exchanging information. They were joined at the hip professionally and also personally. Angleton liked Philby as more than just a good friend. He found him, very simply, alluring.

George du Maurier would have found Angleton and Philby parallel characters to Svengali and Trilby in his 1894 book, *Trilby*, in which Svengali dominates, exploits, and seduces Trilby O'Ferrall, a young Irish girl. Philby, a villain by any standards, had a similar controlling influence over Angleton. The latter was content to let this happen. It was at one level almost a hypnotic relationship. Underneath the professional discussions and exchanges of the most sensitive US-UK intelligence lay a deep-rooted affection.

Angleton was Trilby to Philby's Svengali. Behind the hypnotic relationship was the long arm of the Soviet KGB, an organization that had carefully seduced Philby at Cambridge, playing equally hypnotically on both his intellectual vulnerabilities and his sexual preferences. It was a clever strategy that multiplied in kind across four others at Cambridge, victims seduced not just by Marxist-Leninist ideology but also by interlocking sexual orientation decades before more liberal times recognized the integrity of each and every human personality and each person's individual sexual needs. Not so in the 1930s, when homosexuality was not just frowned upon and buried in the deepest closets—it was a crime.

Angleton alighted from his car, and as he entered the restaurant, he was committed, intellectually, professionally, and personally, to divulge to Philby one of the greatest intelligence secrets of the time. It was an event that would have momentous consequences.

Their greeting was one of smiles, a firm handshake, and Philby insisting that "lunch is on His Majesty, King George the Sixth." His comment was both propitious and ironic, given that His Majesty had little time left to live and would die on February 6, 1952, while his daughter, the future Queen Elizabeth II, and her husband, the Royal Navy officer Philip Mountbatten, were on a royal tour in Africa. The spring and summer of 1951 would see dramatic consequences of what was about to be disclosed to Philby.

The cocktail starters were followed by a well-chosen sauvignon blanc that Philby selected to accompany the fish courses that both he and Angleton had chosen.

"Exquisite choice, Kim, first rate. I love your choice in wines."

"My pleasure, James. It's the least we can do to say thank you for all you do for our relationship."

"Well, Kim, I have some critical information for you, your ears only. I know that no one at your embassy knows what I'm about to tell you, not even the ambassador. Just a chosen few in London are in the know, and of course your key people down in Cheltenham."

"Is this GCHQ material then, James?"

"Absolutely, pure gold, and fully corroborated by our Australian friends."

There was a pause. A pin could have dropped.

"A great joint operation by your key code breakers, Kim, aided and abetted by the community."

Philby took a deep breath, raised himself a little from his chair, looked around the restaurant to ensure that no one was within earshot, and clasped his hands together.

"Venona, Kim, Venona. Have you heard the name?"

"No, James, what is Venona? A program, an operation, a code name?"

"All of the above, Kim. All of the above. Your people are as good as ever, true Bletchley Park heirs and successors. The best of the very best. Plus great work by our Aussie friends."

"I'm all ears, James." Philby was transfixed.

"Well, Venona is the program name for the penetration of the KGB's communications network. Venona reads their traffic."

"My God." Philby almost exploded. "You're serious."

"Never more so, Kim." Your people have been reading their stuff, plus a defector in Australia has added a piece to the communications puzzle."

"What's the puzzle look like?" Philby interjected.

"It's scary, Kim, scary. You Brits have a serious problem. There's a bad apple or two in your barrel."

"Tell me more." Philby was instantly becoming nervous. The phrase *bad apple* resonated. He instantly knew that the Americans knew that the British had a traitor or more in their midst.

"Venona and the defector confirm that there is at least one British KGB spy in London, buried at the top of your organization. A massive danger to our mutual security.

"Before I left Langley, I met with the DD for plans, Allen Dulles. We had a long discussion about the implications and our relationship with MI6 and your government. I'm meeting in the morning with the director and Dulles before they leave to meet with the president. They want my damage assessment. President Truman has caught wind from one of his military people at the agency. Not good. Your PM is going to be a very angry man when Truman discusses all this with him."

Clement Attlee, the British prime minister until Winston Churchill succeeded him in October 1951, was in the middle of this firestorm at a time when a general election in Britain would shortly return Churchill to Number 10 Downing Street. He was not a happy man when the director of MI6, the director of MI5, and the chairman of the Joint Intelligence Committee gave him the very bad news.

"Who and where, James?"

There was a pause as Angleton's steely eyes met Philby's.

"Most likely London, in the very heart of your setup—the JIC or MI6."

"How close is Venona to a revelation?" Philby asked with a tremor in his voice.

"Very close, very close indeed. It's all about your people piecing one and two together and making three. A question of time, Kim, just a question of time, and we'll have whoever in the bag."

"Excellent, excellent," responded Philby, with a nervous quiver in his voice.

"I'll keep you totally in the picture, Kim, and let you know what the president says after the meeting with my director."

Angleton changed the subject to the role of the Australian SIS and how it managed to be so effective with a relatively small number of people and limited investment. Philby's mind wandered to the point of inattention. A more astute person who had not been plied with three martinis at this point in the luncheon might well have noticed that not only was Philby distracted, he clearly was very nervous about something.

Angleton's commitment to Philby and their years of close cooperation now worked against his detecting that what he had told Philby had rattled him. He was oblivious to Philby's internal mental stress. Philby's reactions in normal circumstances, with an American who was not close to him in ways that Angleton was, might well have set off alarm bells. Was Philby displaying the very simple and basic reactions of being informed of the prospect of a Soviet spy or spies inside the heart of British intelligence? Philby showed no such reactions. To a more perceptive and independent American observer, Philby's reactions would have raised flags.

Angleton and Philby prepared to leave the restaurant. Angleton put up his right hand gently to encourage Philby to sit for just a moment longer. He put his hand to his inside suit pocket and retrieved a small piece of folded paper. Angleton looked at Philby and said in a very low voice, "You never saw this, Kim. For your eyes only."

He handed the paper to Philby.

There was a single name on the rather crumpled piece of paper.

Philby gulped.

"I have to keep this, Kim. You never saw it. Time to go. I've got to get back to headquarters. The DD wants to meet with me."

"Thank you, James. Thank you for the heads up. I'm horrified and embarrassed."

"Things happen, Kim; we both know that. Who knows what's motivated him."

Angleton held out his hand to Philby in the parking area and shook his hand with a firm and friendly grip.

"We'll work this, Kim. Never fear."

Philby, for once, was silent, inwardly shocked, and his reticence at their departure was motivated by a deep-seated inward fear, to the point of panic.

As he headed toward the British embassy, only one thought was on his mind.

"If they know about him, who else do they know about?"

As the guard ushered Philby through the embassy gates, that one word on the piece of paper sent a shiver down his spine.

That one word would start a maelstrom in British intelligence.

"Maclean, Maclean, Maclean."

Philby headed to his office. He closed the door. Sat for a few minutes. He then picked up his internal phone and dialed Burgess's extension number.

"We need to talk urgently. Change any evening plans that you have, Guy. We'll talk at the house. That's all. No more."

"But what...?" Burgess said at the other end.

"Enough. No more talk here. Head back to the house as soon as you can at the close of play."

Philby put the phone down. He leaned back in his chair, and internally he realized that Maclean was not the only one in great danger: how long would it be before the magical "Venona" revealed all? Was he in danger of exposure? Was a trap being set? Had Angleton in fact set him up, on higher-up direction? His mind wandered. Guilt set in about actions that may have raised suspicion. He dwelled on his 1934 marriage to the Austrian communist, Litzi Friedmann, who had been born Alice Kohlmann. Had their marriage and 1946 divorce come back to haunt him?

July 1951 was a month of reckoning in Washington, DC.

CHAPTER 9
RAPACITY WITHOUT REMORSE

As Philby closed his study door, Burgess was looking frayed and nervous—rightly so. What news was Philby about to impart?

"They know, Guy," were the first words out of Philby's mouth.

"They know Donald Maclean is batting on a different side. I had it from the horse's mouth today. They know there's at least one other, maybe more. Angleton thinks it's only a question of time."

"How do they know, for God's sake?" exclaimed Burgess.

"It doesn't matter, Guy. They know. It's that simple."

Philby had decided between leaving the embassy and arriving home that perhaps it was a setup of a different color. Was Venona a trap, a means to ferret out the likes of him, Burgess, and Maclean? Was this a subtle ploy of the American counterintelligence organization? Were the FBI and MI5 behind this? He did not know. He was in a total world of speculation.

"Guy, I've given it a lot of thought. The answer's simple."

Burgess was ashen white.

"What are you saying, Kim? What's the simple answer?"

"You need to go, Guy, and soonest. You need to go before they arrest you."

"Where?"

"Moscow, Guy, Moscow. You and Maclean need to get out quickly. I've thought long and hard about all this. I'm seeing our man tonight. I sent him a coded message from the call box down the street. He needs to know that we're all in danger."

"Prepare to make an excuse to go to London. Anything. Family emergency or maybe a legitimate embassy business issue. Something that your boss will buy. Anyway, you have to get out quickly and head for Europe and let our people take you from there. I'll talk with him tonight. Stay up until I return and Guy—no drinking. Stay sober. While I'm gone, please don't hit the bottle."

Burgess was in a state of shock.

The ramifications of what Philby had disclosed and ordered him to do hit home.

"I'm meeting with him shortly. I'll need to leave soonest. I'm worried in case they've already got surveillance on us. I'm going to be extra careful. Our man knows that. Guy, get some rest. When I return, be ready to talk. Please, no drinking. A lot's at stake."

The rest became history, at one level; at another it became a sordid piece of escapism from less-than-efficient counterintelligence by both the British and American security services, MI5 and the FBI. Venona was real enough. If it had been shared with those responsible for taking quick and effective legal action against the worst traitors in modern British history, the outcome could have been very different. There was little that regular law enforcement could do to prevent Burgess and Maclean from slipping through the net to Moscow. Scotland Yard's Special Branch was in the dark. The FBI was equally ill informed. Sources and methods could easily have been protected. Round-the-clock surveillance, phone tapping, mail intercepts, and a deep investigation into Burgess's and Maclean's pasts would have shown vulnerabilities to be exploited by the KGB.

Philby returned from his meeting, one executed with consummate tradecraft, with almost no real direct contact—but rather exchanges between the Russian and Philby in the men's room of a local bar. Handwashing has virtues besides good hygiene.

The Russian checked to ensure that none of the stalls were occupied and in just a few short sentences, in the lowest voice, told Philby that Burgess should leave immediately via Europe for Moscow. KGB London would ensure that Maclean was warned, too, and his escape assured before arrest could follow at any time soon. Philby was told how. Tomorrow was Burgess's last day in Washington. He had to leave immediately for the Moscow sanctuary and the welcoming arms of his KGB controllers.

Philby told Burgess to essentially pack his bags—time to say goodbye.

Neither slept that night. Philby's mind was running at a hundred miles an hour. Burgess was in a daze, wondering what lay ahead in Moscow: the end of his privileged life—and the beginning of what?

As the sun came up and the Washington, DC, area came to life, Philby was up early, drinking coffee as if it were his last taste of his favorite morning elixir.

Burgess was packed and ready to go.

Philby had thought hard.

A fast train to New York City and a flight to Europe. Burgess would call in sick. He had plenty of cash. He needed to leave soonest.

Breakfast was perfunctory. Philby debated in his mind whether or not to drive Burgess to Union Station for the train to New York City. He determined that since he was used to driving Burgess because of his heavy drinking habits, driving him was not out of the ordinary. Calling a cab would have its vulnerabilities.

On the way to Union Station, Philby stressed various tradecraft countersurveillance precautions. He emphasized the need to act normally and not to communicate with anyone.

"Zero phone calls, Guy. Got it?"

Burgess nodded agreement.

They parted company somewhat peremptorily at Union Station. Burgess had his clear marching orders. He was not to deviate.

Philby clutched Burgess's hand and then hugged him. He looked around furtively and told Burgess to depart quickly and take the very first express train to New York City.

Philby breathed a sigh of relief as he drove back to the house, composed himself, drank more coffee, and decided how he would handle Angleton. They were scheduled to meet for a late lunch after the White House meeting when the CIA director would inform the president of Venona's latest exposures, none of which boded well for the special relationship.

Philby became unnerved when he reached his embassy office. His secretary informed him that Angleton had called and wanted to change their venue. He requested that Philby visit him at CIA headquarters at 1400 hours. Philby took a deep breath and asked her to call back to the agency and respond in the affirmative.

As Philby drove up the George Washington Memorial Parkway and then deviated down Route 123 to the CIA main entrance, he was sweating. His blood pressure was elevated, his face was reddened when he looked in the car mirror, and his heart rate was racing. He was well on time, so he pulled over at a gas station to compose himself, stretch his legs, and think about his options. What would Angleton be offering?

Angleton greeted him in the main entrance lobby of the CIA. His face was stark and worried looking.

"Come on up, Kim, we've got some tough issues to resolve."

Philby looked at Angleton, "More bad news, then?"

"Yes, I'm afraid so, and you and I need to talk privately. Very privately."

Angleton's door closed within the innermost sanctum of the CIA.

CHAPTER 10

A RECKONING

"It's not good, Kim," said Angleton. "In fact it's the ugliest I've ever seen. Have a seat. Would you like coffee, or tea?"

"I may need something stronger, but I'm fine for now, thank you, though. I'm all ears."

"Well, first off, the briefing to the president went down like a lead balloon. After the usual morning briefing on current intelligence things, the director told him the Venona story."

"And...?" asked Philby.

"He's normally cool, calm, and collected. This is the man who ordered the attacks on Hiroshima and Nagasaki. He's not one to squirm at hearing bad news, and he certainly can make the most demanding of decisions. But this hit home—hard."

"What happened?"

"Evidently he found it difficult to believe any of it at first, and he spent several minutes reciting the great things that the Brits did during and immediately after the war. He was skeptical. 'Show me the evidence,' he ordered. The DD told me that when the intercepted material was laid out in front of him, with a synopsis of the critical bits that showed beyond all doubt that you have spies working at the top of British intelligence and in your Foreign Office, he not only believed what he was shown, he also became angry."

"Was his anger vented in any direction?"

"Kim, it was the material that's likely been given away. Your JIC has been a sieve, and frankly, a lot of highly sensitive projects that we have shared with six and your Cabinet Office have gone over to the other side, through KGB handlers. No question, Kim, no question. Incontrovertible."

"What did he decide?"

"He didn't. Like the great president that he is, he asked for the best advice and direction."

"And...did the director advise and direct?" asked Philby in a direct, almost obsequious tone.

Philby fidgeted in his seat and became red in the face. What else was coming?

"We have to be very careful. Until we know the full scope of who, what, how much, and when, and worse still, in light of the ongoing operations by Venona's British spies, the director and the team here are not only going to be extremely cautious in their relationships with your people, Kim, they are also closing the doors for a while—until this unholy mess is cleared up."

"What will that take? What can I do to help?"

Philby's voice was less than sincere. He was dumbfounded and searching in his mind to say the right things, to appease Angleton and appear above all else innocent of any of the claims now leveled at the British.

"There are more bad apples in the barrel, Kim; it's not only very clear but also of deep concern that we may not know exactly who for a while yet. We are close. One key defector that the Aussies have is spilling the beans. Our issue, my issue, is what are our internal best next moves? This is where I must not only be frank but also issue a warning, Kim—yes, a warning to you, my best and most trusted British friend and colleague, who I will do anything for."

"I need that coffee, please, James," interjected Philby, his only way to not only lower the tempo but also give himself time to think about what he would say.

Angleton buzzed his secretary for the much-needed caffeine.

His trusted secretary left the two coffees and closed the door.

Angleton took a deep breath, looked at Philby, and said in a low voice, "Kim, you're a suspect."

"What?" Philby gasped.

"By definition, Kim. You're at the heart of the matter, the very inner workings of everything that we secretly know and keep closest. You and several others, too, by definition. Be warned, please, Kim."

"What are you really saying, James?" Philby said in a shocked voice.

"I'm telling you, Kim, that you're on our short list. It's only a matter of time before the security system will click into gear, both here and undoubtedly back in London, once your JIC chairman and the head of MI5 talk with your PM. The president has a call-in tomorrow with the prime minister after the morning briefing in case there is any updated material that shows us more than we know already. That's what's driving the timing in the White House. My director does what the president wants. He's adamant. If there are British spies on the loose, then the special relationship has to be suspended, of sorts, until we jointly know the worst. The facts will speak for themselves. This could not have come at a worse time."

"And us, James, us?" Philby said almost in a begging tone.

"I trust you implicitly, Kim," responded Angleton, "but I've been given my marching orders."

"What are those?"

"Close down contact, Kim, close down contact. We cannot meet again until this ungodly mess is cleared up. You're a suspect, good friend, you're a suspect."

"No more meetings?"

"No more meetings, Kim, and let me tell you one critical piece that I will share with you."

Philby almost dropped his coffee cup.

"Burgess, Guy Burgess, at your embassy. He's on the top of the list with Maclean. For goodness' sake, don't breathe a word. Your people are being told by the most secretive back channels. It may take time to unearth him and others. Your MI5 and British law enforcement will have to act, and soonest."

"Oh no, I don't believe it. Burgess, of all people," Philby exclaimed in the most insincere of tones.

"Yes, and others too."

Angleton's telephone rang. His secretary reminded him that the director of operations wanted to see him urgently.

"You'll have to excuse me, Kim—the DO boss wants me immediately. Most likely about all this. I'll escort you out. Let's go, and I hope that you'll be out of the woods soonest."

"Me too, James, me too. This is a bombshell."

As Angleton shook hands with Philby in the main entrance lobby of the CIA, Philby had an inexorable feeling and intuition that he would never step inside the CIA's hallowed precincts ever again.

He was 100 percent correct in his assessment.

"Good luck, dear friend," said Angleton. "We'll come through. Mark my words."

"We'll be back in business." They shook hands.

Philby was indeed near the top of the suspect list.

This was the last time that they would meet until several years later, in the Middle East, in Beirut. The Angleton-Philby relationship was too entrenched, too personal, and too abiding to be torn apart by this humiliating scandal for Anglo-American relations.

There was perhaps much more to their relationship than what we know from official records. What happened next, between May 1951 and the assassination of President Kennedy in 1963, bears careful scrutiny. The twelve-plus years that followed the parting of ways at the CIA were perhaps more significant and earth shattering than the scandal that was about to erupt in the United Kingdom: the exposure of Burgess and Maclean and all that followed.

Kim Philby left the CIA for the last time, returned to the embassy, and awaited messages from London. None came. It was late in the day in London. "Tomorrow will be," in the words of Margaret Mitchell, "another day."

Tomorrow would indeed determine Philby's fate.

In July 1951, Philby resigned from MI6 after eleven years of service. In 1955, after an exhaustive but totally ineffective investigation of Philby's roles and relationships, he was exonerated. He secretly continued to work for MI6, mainly in Beirut. In January 1963, after further investigation, the hammer came down, but in a horrendously organized and executed way. Instead of British law enforcement taking absolute charge and sending a well-trained and organized team to extract Philby from Beirut, amateur hour continued inside the MI6 temple. The person sent to interview, challenge, and apprehend Philby merely tipped him off, and before law enforcement could strike, he was in a safe haven in Moscow. On January 23, 1963, Philby made his escape from Beirut.

People like Alan Nunn May and Klaus Fuchs, the British atomic spies, were apprehended. Philby had escaped detection and apprehension for all those years after he left Washington, DC, and officially resigned from MI6, a scandalous outcome that would take decades to repair in the eyes of many in the United States.

What happened between July 1951 and the period following President Kennedy's assassination bears close scrutiny. Indeed the key to the Philby-Angleton relationship may well lie in these critical years before Philby's defection, followed by Angleton's actions in the United States in the critical years 1962–1963 during the Bay of Pigs fiasco, the Cuban Missile Crisis, and the ultimate tragedy on November 22, 1963. The years after, when Angleton was at the height of his power and influence at the CIA, have to be seen in the context of these precursor years, when Philby and Angleton were able to meet and do what they did totally uninhibited by US and British security. The true nature of that relationship is crucial for the post-Washington period in Philby's career before defection—and what he likely did for the Soviet Union when ensconced in Moscow. The damage that Angleton wrought while head of CIA counterintelligence was absolutely enormous. Where did the abiding "Philby factor" fit into this tapestry of intrigue and treachery? The story now begins.

CHAPTER 11
NOTHING IS EVER QUITE WHAT IT APPEARS

The great poet T. S. Eliot wrote in his *Four Quartets* the following majestic lines:

> What might have been is an abstraction
> Remaining a perpetual possibility
> Only in a world of speculation.

And he concludes,

> Time past and time future
> What might have been and what has been
> Point to one end, which is always present.

In the case of the Angleton-Philby relationship, there is considerable scope for speculation. However, there are critical signs and hard evidence that what they did and would do, together and individually, combined to create an ever-present set of effects that persisted until Angleton was summarily dismissed from the CIA and Philby died in Moscow. The past, present, and future did indeed meld together to create a forever that was not just present in their individual lives but also had an overall impact on major world events.

After Burgess's and Maclean's defections in 1951, Philby's defection from Beirut in 1963, and Director of Central Intelligence William Colby's firing of Angleton on Christmas Eve 1974, there are twenty-three years of interconnected events. These lead a reasonable person, when examining events, motivations, and past actions, to conclude that there are several very credible and possible explanations and conclusions to be drawn about both the connections of these two men and what lay behind what is very clearly a deeply rooted and abiding relationship.

The key question is, Were the same puppet masters in Moscow pulling both their strings for the duration of their careers and lives? There was a possibility that Angleton was indeed a KGB agent—not just of the most odious kind, like Kim Philby, but the ultimate highly clever and evasive Soviet spy who played a game that was far more complex, cunning, effective, and interactive than anything that resembled the games of the Cambridge Five, of which Philby is clearly the exemplar. This scenario then begs the question whether they knew of each other's perfidy or, totally unknowing of the other's treachery, were controlled in two totally separate ways, with different objectives, modi operandi, and attendant tradecraft by their Soviet handlers.

The KGB that recruited the Cambridge Five and potentially James Jesus Angleton would have been dissociated, if our understanding of Cold War KGB operations is accurate. The KGB of Andropov would undoubtedly have kept the operations in highly compartmentalized separate parts of the KGB. It is also possible that Angleton, deluded by his own sense of self, his self-importance, conceit, and arrogance, may have allowed himself, via his Israeli Mossad connections, to have been ostensibly recruited by the KGB while remaining a loyal American: a double, in effect. The Mossad saw in Angleton their ultimate American ally. There is no question about this whatsoever. The memorials in Israel to Angleton testify to this.

The worst-case scenario, that Angleton was recruited like Philby as a direct agent, still bears consideration. This is based on the incontrovertible and unbelievable damage that Angleton did as head of counterintelligence at the CIA—until direct intervention by no less than the CIA director. There are alternative explanations based on his character and psychological aspects. His conduct raises a fundamental question about his motivation.

This scenario is reinforced by the blatant, inaccurate, and foolhardy accusations that Angleton sowed about key American allies. What would have been the KGB's operational objectives if this is true? One key and overarching objective would have been the destabilization of the NATO alliance. This stratagem would have been clever in the extreme, since it would manifestly have had the appearance of counterintelligence rectitude from Angleton, while in fact he used the system to undermine its very self.

The cleverness and irony of this scenario are somewhat diabolical. Angleton contested that British prime minister Harold Wilson was a Soviet recruit, that his rival for the premiership, Hugh Gaitskell, was killed in 1963 to prevent him from challenging Wilson. This all seems extremely convoluted, perhaps excessive. However, if you were running things in Moscow in the 1960s, nothing would have been more effective than to have the powerful and unrestrained American head of counterintelligence making false claims against well-established Western leaders.

Angleton made claims that the head of the British security and counterintelligence service, MI5, Sir Roger Hollis, was also a Soviet agent. Was this Angleton paranoia at its worst, or the manifestation of an extremely clever and odious KGB plan?

Angleton went further afield than the United Kingdom—to Australia, Canada, and Germany, where he generated similar false claims against key leaders: in effect disinformation based on unsubstantiated evidence.

Creating doubt in people's minds about the loyalty of their leadership would have been a primary KGB objective. How directly involved with Soviet entities was Angleton in this disinformation and destabilization campaign? Angleton had enormous power, the scope of which came to light only after his professional dismissal and later death. The investigation by the Church Committee showed clearly that Angleton had been running domestic spying operations from the CIA, all totally illegal.

Whatever the fundamental truth of all the above, the key fact is that Angleton knew no bounds; he became a law unto himself, out of control, and a man who, whatever his motivation, was not being internally reviewed and checked. Who was checking on the very man who led CIA counterintelligence? The answer is no one. He had carte blanche to do whatever he wanted, and indeed he did.

Was Angleton simply paranoid, or is there another story?

The story now unfolds.

CHAPTER 12

GAME, SET, AND MATCH

J. Edgar Hoover led the FBI for nearly a half century, from 1924 to 1972. During the critical period in question, leading to President Kennedy's assassination in November 1963, the FBI had taken the lead in US domestic counterintelligence, counterespionage, and countersabotage investigations. However, the relationship between CIA counterintelligence and FBI counterintelligence was far from satisfactory. In the midst of this situation was none other than James Jesus Angleton, a law unto himself and totally at variance and noncommunicative with the FBI. J. Edgar Hoover was not a happy man.

It is a chilly January morning in Washington, DC, in 1963. The day is Friday, January 19. Four days later, on Wednesday, January 23, 1963, a significant event will occur not unrelated to what is about to transpire.

The deputy director of the FBI, Clyde Tolson, tells his FBI driver to return to the McLean Squash and Tennis Club in two hours, at 13:30. It is shortly before 11:30 as he grabs his tennis gear and racquet and heads into the club.

As deputy director of the FBI, he has decades of experience with his illustrious boss, J. Edgar Hoover. They have worked together in close unison since Tolson became deputy director in 1930. Tolson, like Hoover, has seen it all: through the law enforcement troubles of the 1930s, the huge challenges of World War II, and now the Cold War and an aggressive Soviet Union, with the KGB operating aggressively on American soil.

Angleton has a much easier ride from CIA headquarters. As he parks his car at the club, he notices Clyde Tolson leaving his marked government car and enters the club.

In the changing rooms, Angleton and Tolson have a polite but not exactly friendly handshake. Angleton lets him know that they have a court for one hour, from 11:30 to 12:30, and that he has booked a table for lunch.

They rally for about ten minutes or so on one of the fine indoor courts, almost alone except for four ladies playing doubles.

Tolson wins the toss and elects to serve first.

"Let battle commence," quips Angleton.

These are ironic words. Tolson is fit and healthy and well coached in 1960s-style tennis. Angleton is not very fit: he needs to lose several pounds, he gets out of breath easily, and he quickly needs a rest at the three-games interval. It is already three games to love in Tolson's favor. Angleton's drinking and eating habits are catching up.

Tolson is gracious as Angleton serves for the fourth game. However, his natural talent prevails. Angleton quickly succumbs in the first set, a somewhat embarrassing six-games-to-love win for the FBI's deputy director.

The second set is equally amateur hour for Angleton, with only one game to his credit—solely because of double faults in one game by Tolson, who is experimenting with a new spin serve. The set ends six games to one. Tolson pats Angleton on the back and shakes his hand, and they retire to shower and change.

Lunch will have a very different flavor from what Angleton anticipates.

The club is quiet, and both can speak without lowering their voices or looking around furtively to check who may eavesdrop.

After ordering a fairly modest starter and main course, with just ice water to drink, Tolson opens the dialogue after initial pleasantries. This meeting is official—"On Uncle Sam, and the bureau," comments Tolson.

Tolson goes straight to the point.

"James, we in the bureau value enormously what you do at the agency, particularly in your realm, counterintelligence, where I have particular interests and ones that the director has specifically charged me to oversee."

He pauses for a drink of ice water.

"I'm here to ask for your direct cooperation in several domains and regarding specific individuals whom the bureau regards as pressing and urgent threats to our national security. There are blurred lines of responsibility, and I want to ensure that we cooperate fully so that one or more of the individuals who are on our short list of the most dangerous to our well-being don't slip though the net because of a failure or breakdown in communications between the bureau and the agency."

"I see," says Angleton somewhat guardedly. "Is there a problem? I wasn't aware of one, or maybe I'm missing something."

Angleton is clearly defensive, and Tolson strikes further.

"Before we get into the specifics of who, what, and how, I have another, more pressing issue to discuss. One that I think needs your input and perhaps urgent attention."

Before Angleton can respond, the waiter serves two hot bowls of clam chowder with bread rolls and departs.

Tolson fires a sudden verbal bullet.

"Philby, Harold Kim Philby. I believe that you know him really quite well, James?"

There is a pause.

"You've worked with him during and since World War II—so our British counterparts tell us."

Angleton is nonplussed. Where is this coming from, and where is it going, and why?

"Kim, you knew him well, yes?"

"Of course—I've worked on and off with Kim Philby during and since the war. I'm sure that you know the story? Resigned from MI6 over the Burgess and Maclean scandal; there was an enormous, long-lasting investigation, and he was totally vindicated. In fact I believe one of their ministers rose in the House of Commons to say just that. Philby was innocent of wrongdoing or association with Burgess and Maclean."

"Well, not quite so, James, I regret to say."

"What do you mean? Do you know something that I don't know?"

"Probably, given your reaction."

"What is it?"

"We're close to our opposite numbers in Britain, MI5, totally separate from the people that you've worked with."

"And…?" queried Angleton.

"Well, the bad news is that a recent and highly reliable defector has fairly and squarely confirmed that Philby has been a Soviet agent for years, recruited while at Cambridge by the KGB, together with Burgess and Maclean. He's it, James; Philby is the 'third man.' He's worked for the Soviets all this time: before, during, and after the war."

"Oh my God. And so what's happening? Where is he? What are the British doing?"

"MI5 are in charge, but because Philby is right now in Beirut, they're letting your friends in MI6 go out and haul him back, or that's at least what our liaison in London expects based on all that we've been told. Philby had caused the utmost damage, and my boss and the attorney general have given the president the bad news. Pretty ugly situation. And President Kennedy has his plate full right now in the aftermath of the Cuban Missile Crisis and the Bay of Pigs fiasco. Your agency is not his favorite right now, James. I'm sure that you know that without me rubbing salt in the wound."

"Oh my God, Philby, Kim Philby. All these years—I can hardly believe it."

An impartial onlooker listening in might have speculated that Angleton's reaction was not just bland but perhaps even insincere.

"There's a linkage between the Philby affair and why I'm really here, James, why we in the bureau need your help and cooperation."

"Tell me more, Clyde. What do you need?"

"We have a short list, less than twenty names right now, of people we want to know about twenty-four seven: where they are, what they're doing, who they're meeting with and why, and most of all, what they're planning on doing next and with whom."

"How does the agency fit in? Isn't this your territory? Domestic counterintelligence and counterespionage?"

"Not quite. I think that you understand. The agency is involved. You have your ways and means. The key point is this. Several of the people, US citizens, and in one case a flip-flop US-Soviet citizen, are on our radar because they are overseas, and we believe they are threats to national security, and worst of all, to the president of the United States."

"What's the tie-in? What are the connections?"

"Cuba, the Soviets and, ironically, dissatisfied and angry anti-Castro Americans tied in with the wrong people on the Cuban side of things—the anti-Castro extremists who want to keep the fires burning, who want the attack on Castro's Cuba to become real."

"How are these people tied in with the Soviets? There's a contradiction. Moscow feeds Castro."

"Yes, but the Soviets have figured out how to turn anti-Kennedy and anti-Castro sentiment into a positive, to turn Americans and their surrogates against their own government because of a misplaced understanding of the dynamics of what's happened since the president resolved the missile crisis with Khrushchev."

"I see: complex, nasty, and potentially effective."

"Yes indeed, and there are others, far less volatile and highly respectable, who will sign up for an aggressive stance against Cuba, and they are, simply, what Dwight Eisenhower called the 'military-industrial complex.'"

"Isn't this over the top?"

"No. Big business, the major defense contractors make money out of this very sort of scenario."

"To the point of challenging established policy? Come on!"

"No, James, that's not the point. We at the bureau know about those people, and they are mainly in the South, who are aligned with Cuban factions that run against what the president and his administration regard as the best interests of US national security,"

"And…?"

"Because President Kennedy does not want third parties and their surrogates running amok with Cuba and feeding directly into Soviet hands opportunities to destabilize US-Soviet relations after the missile crisis. That's it, in a nutshell. We at the bureau want twenty-four seven watch on these various 'no-gooders' who may be the instruments for people who will stay out of the limelight, but, and here's the point, who have the financial wherewithal and anti-Kennedy sentiments to upset this apple cart."

"I see. And you think the agency can help?"

"Absolutely, without a shadow of a doubt. Your input, sources, and methods are critical. We don't want you to and certainly don't expect you to share highly sensitive CIA eyes-only data. But, and here's the 'but,' James, we do want you to share the analyzed end product, the output. How you get it, et cetera, that's your business, not ours."

"I get it. So what do you want? Hard-core things? What?"

"We have a list of people that we will share with you. People that we are watching constantly, but often we lose them. They go out of our scope. We don't know where they are, who they are with, and what they may be up to."

"OK, this seems fair enough. You'll let me have your list?"

"Yes. It's sensitive. Parts of it are classified. Don't want to hand anything over here. My director wants this to be all official, above board, bureau to agency. Nothing under the table."

"I see."

"So we need your full cooperation, James, as director of CIA counterintelligence."

They finish their dessert, an apple strudel with vanilla ice cream, and both order coffee, black, with no sugar or cream.

Clyde Tolson then looks at Angleton over the top of his coffee cup.

"I do have one person that I want to talk about."

"OK, I'm all ears, Clyde."

"Lee Harvey Oswald. You know all about him from your Moscow people, I assume?"

"Yes, I'm familiar."

"Former US marine, trained sharpshooter and sniper, went over to the Soviet Union, gave up his US citizenship, took out Soviet citizenship, and disappeared into the ether from what the bureau can see. Then he reappears. Yes, he decides that the Soviet Union is not for him, and he wants to come back, but how, where, and when? The bad news is that the one piece of reliable intelligence we have is that he's headed for Mexico—in fact the capital, Mexico City."

"OK, and what do you want?"

"Clear, reliable, unadulterated intelligence about Lee Harvey Oswald's movements. We have no reliable pieces to the puzzle that explain who else he's engaged with, and why. We can speculate. One, that the Soviets may have infiltrated him back into Mexico to start work with the Cubans there and possible disaffected Americans—the rather insidious scenario I raised earlier, where the so-called good and the definitely bad mix and match with the end result that the president's policy toward both Cuba and the Soviet Union is destabilized."

"I see. I am sure that we can help."

"Specifics, James?"

"I'm not at liberty to go into detail. Just say that we have ways to track and keep an eye on Lee Harvey Oswald in Mexico City."

"Good, very good, and similarly with the cast of characters that we will send over to you in the classified pouch."

"Yes."

"Thank you, James. My director will be delighted when I report back. Will you brief your director?" Tolson was referring to John A. McCone, who was director of the CIA from November 1961 to April 1965, during the Cuban Missile Crisis and the later assassination of President Kennedy.

"Yes, and I will go through our deputy director for plans. He's Richard Helms, an agency stalwart. I can't go straight to the top. I'll run it all by the DD plans first."

"Good, very good. Thank you, James. I hope you enjoyed lunch?"

"Yes, indeed, thank you. Excellent. This is a good place to meet."

"Before we leave, one thing. Philby."

Angleton's ears pricked up.

"I'm not straying into your business, but given that you were very close to Philby—and I am sure had contact with him while he's been working in Beirut, albeit undercover for MI6—if you think of anything that we can pass on to our friends in MI5, I would be most grateful. Philby is a very bad lot: the worst of the worst. Anything that you have can help. Where he might move to if he's suspicious that the game is up, where he hangs out in his spare time when he's either doing his journalism work or undercover things for your opposite numbers, all would help."

Angleton winced.

"If he gets wind that the game is up, he may get out, just as his two partners in crime did, Burgess and Maclean. I hope to God that the British act quickly now we have the goods on the devil."

Tolson's FBI driver came alongside the club entrance. Tolson shook Angleton's hand, smiled, and thanked him for his commitment of future cooperation.

Angleton struggled to find a smile, bade him farewell, and watched as the deputy director of the FBI headed back to headquarters, seemingly happy with the outcome of lunch and a game of tennis that was best forgotten.

As the government car departed, Angleton stood transfixed for several minutes. One person dominated his thoughts. That person was Harold Kim Philby.

Five days later, on Wednesday, January 23, 1963, Philby left Beirut and was next seen in Moscow. He had successfully defected, prima facie forewarned by a visit from an MI6 official who came to Beirut to further question Philby and accuse him of treachery. He departed either by a Soviet merchant ship, the most likely exit plan, or via the Syrian border. MI6 had bungled the whole operation, or at least apparently so. He escaped arrest and a trial in Britain that perhaps the MI6 leadership regarded as more destabilizing for British intelligence than just letting him go into the arms of his Soviet paymasters.

Where did Angleton fit into all this? Speculation. "A world of specula-tion," to recall T. S. Eliot's fine words.

Whose side was Angleton on? An egotistical own side, forever for Angleton and no one else, even his own country? Or was he the victim of an out-of-control paranoia that knew no bounds, to the point of total self-deception, while causing untold harm? Or worse, was he working all along with Philby and the others for the Soviet Union?

Nineteen sixty-three was a year that may hold answers to these hypoth-eses: more so than all Angleton's remaining years left at the CIA, when he created counterintelligence mayhem, wrecking careers, making totally false accusations, and wasting hugely critical resources, before the final reckoning on that fateful Christmas Eve.

Tragedy was to become part of the Angleton story. His meeting with Deputy Director Tolson was a prelude to what many will consider the most odious of all Angleton's actions. The consequences of these actions even to this day have never been fully appreciated.

There are indeed parallels with 9/11. The scenarios are totally different, yet the critical relationship, or lack thereof, between the CIA and the FBI is tragically similar.

The failure of the CIA to share, completely and in a timely manner, critical intelligence that directly impacted the work of the FBI was, in retrospect, fringing on criminal: a total failure to share vital intelligence that in 1963 might well have forestalled Lee Harvey Oswald and a whole network that was involved.

In 2001 the crucial details of the movements and locations of the 9/11 plotters, and their later associations and correlations as flight trainees at various flight schools in the United States, would have been vital pieces of information for the FBI. If it had received such information from the CIA, there is no doubt whatsoever that the FBI would have instantly implemented intensive round-the-clock surveillance of the 9/11 plotters and their leadership, plus telephone and email tapping and tracking developments at the various flight schools.

The role of James Jesus Angleton in 1963 in the crucial months before the November assassination bears close examination. Whose side was he on? This is not a rhetorical or outlandish question, one posed to create doubt, skepticism, or disharmony. What Angleton did was not reflected in the official transcript of the Warren Commission into the assassination of President Kennedy. Angleton perjured himself in his testimony. In a nutshell, he lied.

Why? That is the question.

His failures with the FBI were egregious. What motivated him?

He completely violated his verbal commitment to the FBI.

J. Edgar Hoover was left in the dark by Angleton's transgressions.

The FBI was struggling to monitor and track the machinations of various internal US activities associated with the strong anti-Castro, and therefore anti-Kennedy, groups. Who was behind them, who was pulling the strings, who was paying the tabs, and what were the political motivations?

It was clear to Director J. Edgar Hoover that, whatever the private philandering of his president, with which he was very familiar, protecting the president was his primary duty. He was undoubtedly aware, too, that all was not well within the White House between President Kennedy and his vice president, the Texan Lyndon Johnson. Although the latter was a fervent advocate of several key social issues, including civil rights, he had serious differences between himself and his president over national security issues. His views on Cuba and the Soviet Union were at variance with President Kennedy's. Other elements within the defense and intelligence community were not only aware of such differences; they were also Lyndon Johnson supporters. The Texan, with strong roots in the South, had a totally different following than his leader, who had a widely differing intellectual and policy perspective on world affairs. Eisenhower's famous military-industrial complex was undoubtedly part of this pro-Johnson ensemble, a recipe for discord if exacerbated by more extreme fringe groups that saw in John Fitzgerald Kennedy the apotheosis of strict anti-Soviet and anti-Cuban policies.

Angleton was in the middle of this mix. He had critical information that Director Hoover badly needed. What happened next is the prelude to tragedy.

CHAPTER 13

SHAKEN, NOT STIRRED, BY THE FBI

Angleton's arrogance, self-assurance, and unassailable position as CIA counterintelligence supremo gave him enormous power, all at the wrong time in US history.

He never fulfilled any of his key commitments to the FBI. In retrospect it is clear that he had no intention of keeping his agreement to share vital national security intelligence to monitor the movements and possible intentions of Lee Harvey Oswald. A key question is, How much did he share with his leadership at the CIA? The evidence below points to very little, if indeed anything. He was a power unto himself, a counterintelligence demigod with unbridled scope to act without either control or oversight. The results were catastrophic. The fine work of Mr. Jefferson Morley of the *Washington Post* has exposed the worst of some of Angleton's transgressions, particularly the written and sworn testimony years afterward of Angleton's personal assistant who handled much if not all of his most sensitive information. We owe a lot to Jefferson Morley.

Meanwhile Philby is rehabilitated by MI6 after he is cleared of any wrongdoing. His KGB masters must have celebrated in Moscow after a public pronouncement of Philby's innocence in the House of Commons by none other than the foreign secretary, Harold MacMillan, much to his later chagrin when Philby was exposed for what he was and had defected to the Soviet Union. Philby is employed in his original journalism work by highly reputable British newspapers, all a cover for his covert work for MI6. In essence it is business as usual, while he remains officially "off the books" but very much still one of the darlings of his MI6 masters.

Philby has prima facie excellent "cover" while operating all the time for the Soviet Union. His time in Beirut after his rehabilitation and before he defected in January 1963 is a crucial period in terms of possible contact and meetings with Angleton.

Angleton had extremely good connections with the Israeli Mossad. This is incontrovertible. What remains an open question is Angleton's detailed travel between the United States and the Middle East between the late 1950s and late 1963, after the assassination of President Kennedy.

Given Philby's rehabilitation, and given his clandestine work out of Beirut for MI6, it is likely that he and Angleton met in Beirut and in other Middle Eastern locations. Given the close proximity of Tel Aviv in Israel to Beirut in Lebanon, it would have been an easy commute either way so that both could meet. They would have met without question, as they always had in the past, in totally nonofficial locations and, given both of their penchants for good food and wine, in quality restaurants.

Philby would have met his KGB controllers in the usual nefarious ways, easily achieved in Beirut in the late 1950s and early 1960s. He ran little risk of counterintelligence detection. Given that Angleton was the head of CIA counterintelligence and would have had contact with the CIA chief of station in Beirut, he could, if he had so desired, have directed counterintelligence operations in Beirut over and beyond other covert HUMINT collection operations.

The role of the Mossad vis-à-vis Angleton remains equivocal. Angleton was their best friend, prima facie. From a Mossad perspective, in the late 1950s, and leading eventually to the 1967 June War, their operational objectives are easy to define. The Soviet Union was engaging clandestinely and overtly with Syria and Egypt while working to isolate King Hussein of Jordan in the Arab anti-Israel camp. Meanwhile Israel, and therefore the Mossad, had its eyes on the West Bank, the Sinai, and the Golan Heights. Military leaders like Moshe Dayan had much more grandiose ambitions to extend even further Israel's "strategic boundaries."

It is March 1961 in Beirut. Philby and Angleton rendezvous at one of their favorite watering holes. Angleton has traveled up from Tel Aviv. Philby has left his apartment after filing a report with the *Economist* in London.

"Kim, I've something important to pass on to your friends in London."

"From the Israelis?"

"No, but I've been keeping them in the loop. They're aware of what I'm about to tell you."

As always, Philby is animated and cannot wait to hear what gems Angleton will disclose.

"Our president is being well advised about Fidel Castro's plans and associations with Moscow. He's taken some convincing. Kennedy is cautious about a lot of our material and recommendations. There are people in DC, in the Pentagon, and at Langley who think that he's too soft on communism."

"And where is he now?" queries Philby.

"He's slowly coming round, along with his brother, the attorney general."

Philby's eyes start to glaze over. What is Angleton about to give away? More gold?

"The agency wants to foment dissent inside Cuba via internal dissidents and our external contacts in Florida and Texas, and a few other choice places that want Kennedy to be more proactive."

"Is Kennedy aware of the internal politics in the American South regarding Cuba?"

"Yes and no, Kim. Given the incredibly close finish in the election between him and Nixon, with Kennedy winning by the tiniest margin, he has a lot of enemies, naturally in the Republican party and within the military establishment."

There is a pause, as if Angleton is deciding whether or not to disclose what he will say next. His trust in Philby gives way, and he cannot hold back.

"I never said this, Kim, you never heard this, but my agency is running internal operations in the US, totally unknown to virtually everyone on Capitol Hill and certainly in the White House. Several key people at Langley are running the show. We've several key sources in Texas and elsewhere that feed us good data on the anti-Cuba dissident movement that will tie in with another major operational plan."

"Operational plan, James?" Philby asks. "Are you doing things with the dissidents?"

"Yes, hell yes, and we keep it very tight. I don't trust Kennedy and his like. However, he has finally bought into one of our key plans. Here goes."

Angleton scans the restaurant furtively, lowers his voice, and says in the lowest of tones, "We're going to mount an OP against Castro and his friends: a huge tie-in between our US-based dissident groups, internal Cuban anti-Castro factions, and us, the paramilitary arm of the agency."

"You're kidding me, James."

"Never been more serious, Kim. Never been more serious. It's about to launch. April 17 is the go date. We're going in with both these loyal guys that we've been working with in the States and the dissidents in Cuba. It's all set."

Philby is temporarily mesmerized. Angleton is giving him not just gold but the keys to the KGB kingdom.

"Bay of Pigs, that's the place—Bay of Pigs. Ever since that son of a bitch Castro came to power in 1959, we've wanted to topple him. Now we're actually going to do it."

"Wow, James, God bless America," an astounded Philby declares with a grimace that hides his real intent.

"I'll say no more, Kim—enough for now. Let the inner circle at Century House know, Kim, but whatever you do, don't transmit anything. You must promise me. Word of mouth only, and only to C and his deputy. They'll love you for this. Talk about a comeback. You'll be a real hero, trust me."

"James, I give you my word, only by word of mouth. I'll sneak in and out of London. Visit choice places on Fleet Street and meet surreptitiously with C or his deputy. I can't afford to have my face recognized in the wrong places."

"That's fine, Kim; I hope this both helps you and also gives six a look into the glass, darkly." Angleton loves to fall back on both his sense of poetry and his Yale knowledge base. He looks at Philby and quotes directly from Corinthians chapter 13, verse 12: "For now we see though a glass darkly; but then face to face: now I know in part; but then shall I know even as also I am known."

"Impressive, James. I'm always amazed at how you have an appropriate quote for every occasion. We Cambridge economics types cannot quote the way you do—amazing, absolutely amazing."

"Thank you, Kim. It was you Brits that gave me the grounding, at Malvern College. Forever grateful."

There is a pause. Philby stares at Angleton.

"By the way, I quoted from the King James Version, the only version worth a damn!" declares Angleton.

"Bravo, James," declares Philby, inwardly thinking that he could quote all right, but it would definitely not be the Bible or poetry. *Das Capital* is Philby's métier.

They part company.

Philby and Angleton would reengage at a later date, and that meeting would be as propitious as this critical meeting of two very evil minds.

The following day Philby meets with his Beirut KGB handler under the guise of meeting a special source: one who feeds Philby the half-truths that Moscow wants him to play back to the innocents in London, in the heart of British intelligence.

"Marvelous, Kim, simply marvelous. Moscow will be not just pleased. They will be overjoyed, indeed overwhelmed. Just what we need to help Castro thwart his American enemies within and without. He will be indebted to us forever."

And so it was.

Between April 17 and 19, 1961, the ill-fated and disastrous Bay of Pigs operation took place, an unmitigated CIA disaster.

The Soviets knew in advance and warned Castro, who was ready in all regards, to extinguish both his internal opponents and the US-led dissidents who were launched at the Bay of Pigs. They would meet a most ignominious and fateful end.

The treacherous hand of Kim Philby would likely play an even more decisive and evil role between April 1961 and his defection in January 1963. In between would unfold the Cuban Missile Crisis and the tragic lead-up to November 1963 and the death of a great American president in Dealey

Plaza, in Dallas, Texas. Meanwhile, Philby had to be sure of one critical fact regarding his own survival during these critical months.

CHAPTER 14

THE J. EDGAR HOOVER FACTOR

The next Philby-Angleton meeting was equally stunning. Philby was a worried man. Like the proverbial cat, Philby was beginning to think that he had nine lives. The question was, Which one was he on? Had he reached number nine? Philby believed that Angleton might be his best guide to where the truth lay. How much time did he have left? He had been accused once, exonerated, and rehabilitated—only because the trusting old boy network in MI6 was naive and unprofessional enough not to dig deeper and deeper into Philby's background and conduct intensive covert counterintelligence against him. MI5 was marginalized. MI6 believed that only it could investigate its own people.

The Al Halabi restaurant in Antelias Square is one of Philby's favorite places to eat and meet his various contacts. He loves the mondardara lentils with rice and caramelized onions. Today he has to decide whether to meet Angleton there or at one of his other two favorite locations, both of which are where Philby and his KGB handler exchange information: the Ichkhanian Bakery, which serves a fusion of Armenian and Lebanese dishes, and the Al Antabli, renowned for its classic Lebanese dishes. He opts for the Al Halabi, mainly because he does not wish to see his Soviet contact possibly having lunch at one of the other two locations. Philby has one objective in mind in light of his latest meeting with his KGB contact.

The question dominating not just Philby's mind but also his masters' in Moscow is, simply, How much time does he have left before the British or the Americans figure out that he is in fact the third man after Burgess and Maclean?

Philby's opening comment after the usual greetings, pleasantries, and catchup is somewhat crass, to the point of lacking any sensitivity. He says, "James, to use a very bad pun, I'm not 'Angling' for an answer, but do you have any more Venona data points for me?"

Angleton stares at Philby momentarily, somewhat taken aback by Philby's direct, leading question. For the first time, the Yale scholar stumbles for words. He composes himself and replies.

"Kim, you're a dear friend, indeed the closest for reasons that we both know, and I often share only with you what I wouldn't even share with colleagues back at Langley."

Philby is relieved. Is Angleton about to give him the latest on Venona? The answer is a resounding yes.

"They're closing in, Kim, closing in. There's definitely another British spy in the MI6 ranks. Time will tell, and I can reassure you that after your full exoneration by British security, the agency has full confidence in you, as always."

"I'm relieved, James. You and I have worked together since we took on and beat the Nazis. This is no time for our relationship, personal as it is, to fall apart because a reliable source is casting aspersions on some British traitor. Hopefully we'll find out who the hell this is and put him, or her, away."

Philby's cunning and hypocrisy are at their darkest and most convincing.

"Yea verily to that, Kim. You, me, and all my people who work for me."

They then indulge themselves in fine Lebanese food, exquisitely prepared and served.

Angleton switches gears after they finish the main course.

"Do you have anything new for me from all your contacts here and throughout the region, after your recent travels?"

Philby insidiously plays back a series of Moscow-created misinformation about Soviet intentions and actions in Syria and Egypt, derived, he claims, from "A1, highly reliable sources" in both countries. He states that the Soviets are not gaining much ground in establishing bases in either country and that both leaderships are skeptical about making overt moves, given both the strength of the US Sixth Fleet in the Mediterranean and the relatively weak position of the Soviet Navy, hemmed in in the Black Sea by the Montreux Convention.

"Excellent, Kim, excellent."

Philby then proceeds to lead Angleton down further rabbit holes.

"Good news for your Israeli friends, James. The Soviets are warning both the Egyptian and Syrian regimes that they may be helpless to intervene if they provoke the Israelis to take aggressive measures."

"My Mossad contacts will be most pleased to hear this, Kim. Moshe Dayan and the hard-liners are more concerned about Soviet reactions than the capabilities of both Egypt and Syria and possibly even Jordan if Hussein decides to run with his Arab cohorts."

Philby inwardly rejoices, knowing from years of past experience that Angleton will now give more than he receives. This is the very nature of their relationship. Angleton is almost spellbound by Philby.

"Let me tell you who my biggest problem is, Kim."

Philby inhales, wondering in a heartbeat what will come next.

"It's called the FBI: J. Edgar Hoover's Federal Bureau of Investigation. They're meddling in our affairs and operations."

"In what ways, James?"

"On paper the FBI runs internal counterespionage in the US, not us. However, we have our special sources and methods, and we're not about to share anything with Hoover and his people. We have our own operations running, Kim, all undercover, inside the United States. It's a very dark secret. Few know about this."

"Well, that's all good, isn't it? Your president must be pleased to have highly secure sources and methods operations against whomever?"

"Yes and no, Kim. Kennedy and his brother play by the federal rule book, particularly his attorney general brother. We don't share a lot, indeed very much, with the White House. They don't need to know."

"Sounds reasonable."

"Well, it is, except that Hoover is on my case—very personal, to the point of weekly harassment."

"About what?"

"He wants a list, with frequent updates, on anyone overseas who they, the FBI, regard as a threat to US security, and Hoover demands that we provide him with the names of such people, their locations, movements, contacts, and likely intentions."

"And..." says Philby.

"He wants all our data on certain individuals, one of whom is a gent called Lee Harvey Oswald."

"I've heard about him," Philby responds.

"Yes, he's a former US marine, trained sharpshooter and sniper, defected to the Soviet Union, marched into our Moscow embassy and declared that he was yielding his US passport and was seeking Soviet citizenship."

"I recall something about all this," Philby says, dissembling, knowing in fact the full story about Oswald and his Soviet activities via his KGB handlers.

"Well, Hoover wants the full scoop on Oswald. Where he is twenty-four seven and who is pulling his strings."

"Maybe fair game?" Philby says in an inquisitive and disarming way.

"Not how I see it. Oswald and the others on Hoover's list are mine and mine alone to keep an eye on. We can track them. We don't want the FBI and Hoover's amateurs playing in my backyard, whether it's overseas or in the continental United States. Key people like Dick Helms and I are on the same page. Keep the FBI out of Langley. I run counterintelligence, not the FBI."

Philby recognizes the political sensitivities of what Angleton is describing and the underlying bureaucratic infighting. His one thought is very simple: all this is for the good of my Soviet paymasters.

"Do you feel confident about retaining control, James, so that the FBI cannot meddle and possibly compromise your sources?"

"Absolutely. We don't tell them a thing. Zero. Hoover's getting nothing from me."

What Angleton does not then disclose to Philby is that he knows all about Lee Harvey Oswald—where he is, with whom he is meeting—and that his return from Moscow to Mexico is closely held in the CIA. He has a key chief of station in Mexico City, in fact, tracking Oswald.

Who had paid for Oswald to learn Russian, a tough language to acquire by any standards?

All this would come to haunt the United States for generations. The Warren Commission and Church Committee were several years away. Even then, not all was revealed. James Jesus Angleton had a lot to answer for.

As they left the restaurant, little did Angleton in his wildest dreams ever consider the possibility that Philby would, within hours, pass all this on to Moscow.

Or alternatively, did he in fact know? Was he part of it all? He would have top cover at Langley, Virginia, for many more years, doing irreparable harm.

Very simply put, whose side was he really on?

His relationship with Philby had been for years more than just that of professional intelligence specialists conducting undercover liaisons. Perhaps herein lay the answer.

CHAPTER 15
THIS IS NOT THE ZIMMERMANN TELEGRAM

In 1917, British naval intelligence, under the leadership of Captain Reginald "Blinker" Hall (later Admiral Sir Reginald Hall), cracked the German code that showed beyond a shadow of a doubt that the Germans were plotting with Mexico, via funding and weapons supplies, to encourage Mexico to invade the southwest United States. The strategic objective of the German foreign minister, Zimmermann, was to distract Woodrow Wilson's government from intervening in the European war on the side of the Allies, led by France and Britain. A war with Mexico would preoccupy the United States.

The British cryptanalysts decoded the key message that was sent from Berlin to the German embassy in Washington, DC, and then on to the German ambassador in Mexico City. Captain Hall's team also managed to deceive the Germans so they would never know what they had achieved or how they had achieved it. The Zimmermann Telegram in due course persuaded President Wilson, Congress, the US press, and the American people that the United States should declare war on Germany.

The challenge that J. Edgar Hoover had requested of Angleton was an issue of major national security. The 1962 Cuban Missile Crisis had gone to the brink of war, though it had been handled brilliantly by President Kennedy, the US Navy, and the critical U-2 flights over Cuba that showed what the Soviet Union was all about. This was before satellites were available to show that the Soviets were building missile launchers.

As 1962 passed into early 1963, there was still serious tension in the international atmosphere. The FBI naturally wanted to track the movements and whereabouts of those the bureau regarded as possible threats to national security.

The list was not exhaustive: in fact it was perfectly manageable in terms of time and resources.

Lee Harvey Oswald was a known quantity. His past record was there for the bureau and the CIA to see clearly.

His movements were known to James Jesus Angleton as head of CIA counterintelligence. Furthermore, the CIA was conducting illicit intelligence operations in the southwest United States with anti-Castro factions and individuals. The Bay of Pigs fiasco had left a deep scar inside the agency, and the Kennedy White House felt deceived and ill advised by its prime HUMINT intelligence agency, one authorized to conduct overseas clandestine operations.

Angleton was now about to ascribe to himself full independent powers to act, or not act, and to control the sources and flow of absolutely critical information regarding a man who had sought and gained Soviet citizenship, then renounced it, and showed intent to return to the United States. Who paid for Oswald's Russian language training remains, to this day, an unknown. There are several options, all totally speculative, without one shred of actual hard evidence.

One possible theme may at times run through what will transpire. This is what may be described as the "good of the service" argument. Secret intelligence services have a habit, perhaps even a tradition, of never wanting to admit mistakes or failed operations—or even publicly recognize that certain personnel are less than stellar, downright incompetent, or worse still, acting in ways that are at total variance with the best interests of national security. It is an institutional malaise of sorts: a covert cover-up, perhaps, by another name and another viewpoint. Leaders of highly classified and covert operations within secret intelligence organizations do not ever want to be, either publicly or behind closed doors, investigated and harangued for their failures. If there are ways to mitigate exposure, minimize negative outcomes, and move on to the next operation, then that will often be the way ahead and the way out. In effect, career-ending events are countered by the most closely guarded internal protective measures.

Angleton enjoyed the benefits of this institutionalized set of behaviors; he also had one incredibly important added privilege, and indeed weapon. As head of counterintelligence, he was the very top person entrusted to oversee and manage not just foreign counterintelligence but also internal CIA counterintelligence. This provided him with an almost unassailable position: one that no one could challenge, with the possible single exception of the director himself, a political appointee confirmed by the US Senate.

Angleton deliberately and willfully failed to send the FBI, and J. Edgar Hoover personally, absolutely critical information regarding the movements and location of Oswald and those with whom he was associating in Mexico City. All this impacted the impending tragedy in Dealey Plaza in Dallas, Texas, with huge lasting ramifications for American politics and the world.

Angleton had a Zimmermann Telegram–type capability and ability to control and determine events and outcomes. What he did, in retrospect, was nothing short of treasonous.

Why?

That is the critical and unanswered question.

What transpired next was very much due to the fine work of Mr. Jefferson Morley, a distinguished *Washington Post* journalist and author of several seminal books. Perhaps most of all, there is a lasting debt to Morley and Dr. John Newman for the interview that they conducted on November 2, 1994, with Jane Roman, Angleton's right-hand person at the CIA who had access to all his material, papers, and files. Jane Roman filed away key documents that were of monumental significance. The interview was transcribed by Mary Bose of the *Washington Post* on November 7, 1994.

There is one other critical event that occurred in January 1963. Kim Philby, the "spy who went into the cold," disappeared from Beirut and defected to Moscow, where he lived until he died in 1988. He had escaped from under the noses of MI6 without the Special Branch of Scotland Yard and the British Security Service being activated to arrest him and return him to Britain to stand trial.

Little or nothing is known about how Angleton reacted when the news of Philby's defection arrived at Langley.

Did he know in advance? Whose side was he on? His side? The other side?

Meanwhile a momentous series of events is in the offing.

Lee Harvey Oswald is in Mexico City with Angleton's full knowledge.

He does not inform the FBI and J. Edgar Hoover.

A key person now becomes critical over the ensuing months.

This is the CIA chief of station in Mexico City, an extraordinarily capable and loyal officer, Winston Scott, who does all the right things.

The tragedy is that between Winston Scott, the FBI, US law enforcement, and the White House is one single person: James Jesus Angleton.

He holds the keys to the kingdom.

CHAPTER 16

A HORSE OF A DIFFERENT COLOR

Lee Harvey Oswald will remain forever in the annals of American history. He is a complex individual, with more yet to be known about him all these years later. The prima facie facts do not match up in light of what transpired. There are more issues yet to be examined and explained.

Now to Mexico City. It is 1963, with critical months to go before John Fitzgerald Kennedy, the thirty-fifth president of the United States, is assassinated in Dallas, on Friday, November 22, 1963, while riding in a motorcade through Dealey Plaza in downtown Dallas, and his state funeral is held in Washington, DC, on Monday, November 25, 1963.

"What's the latest on Oswald?" asks Winston Scott at the morning meeting inside the US embassy in Mexico City.

Scott's staff is animated. They have significant developments to report to their much-liked and much-respected leader.

"Who's first off? Maybe the surveillance operation first?" asks the chief of station.

The small staff looks at one another, and after a pregnant pause, Bill Smeed answers the chief of station.

"Boss, Oswald is the classical enigma. He's all things to all men. We're trying to figure out not just whose side he is truly on but also who is pulling his strings. His puppet masters could be one of two major options, or possibly some combination of both, or indeed a well-planned operation by both."

"I'm all ears, Bill," Scott says.

"Our surveillance team has had its hands full. He's a slippery eel and has moved hotels several times. He's clearly not without funds. Either he's got personal money or he's being funded. He uses cash, sometimes lots of it. He's got access to the bank and clearly has no problem making withdrawals. He eats well, dresses well, and uses taxis without blinking. Where does all this come from? We're working it."

Smeed pauses while the chief of station looks at a classified message from headquarters at Langley, Virginia. He looks up at Smeed. "Keep going, Bill."

"The bad news is that he moves consistently between two locations while living what prima facie looks like the life of a reasonable, well-heeled American tourist without the sightseeing and photograph taking."

"Speaking of photographs, have you taken photographs?" asks the chief.

"Oh yes, lots, mainly at the two key locations."

"I'm all ears. Where?"

"The two embassies, the Soviet embassy and the Cuban embassy. He's got access like he's still a Soviet national. He walks in and out of the Soviet embassy without inhibition or challenge from guards. Clearly he's welcome and stays for protracted periods. These are not consular-type visits, that's for sure. He's doing business, meetings with most likely all the people we don't like. In the case of the Cuban embassy, if he was just there to obtain a visa, his likely legitimate reason for being there in the first place, then he's got a good cover story.

"OK, in the case of the Soviet embassy, are they the usual suspects? The KGB and GRU hoods that we know about?"

"We don't know. He's either practicing classic counterintelligence tradecraft or he has another agenda that we don't fully understand as of right now. However, we have two bits of key surveillance from our tails on him."

Winston Scott sits up straight and is totally animated.

"What are they?"

"He occasionally socializes in local restaurants with both Cuban and Soviet embassy officials. People that we don't know. They're not on our list. He's met with both parties together on two occasions, and we have no data on their intent or the substance of what transpired."

"Is this a new operation, possibly?"

"Yes, because the usual Soviet and Cuban operatives don't seem to be involved. New faces, not on any of our lists, and not seen elsewhere in recent years. We have photos, but they have not yielded much so far.

"Second, he's quite brazen, totally uninhibited. If he were acting sub rosa, we think he'd at least try to shake us off or occasionally feint going to a meeting. He does not rendezvous surreptitiously. No dead letter boxes, no clandestine meetings in well-established meeting points with good counterintelligence procedures. Nothing. He's an open book in these regards."

"So what's your best assessment so far? What do I tell Angleton?"

Smeed turns to Chuck Anderson as the lead person.

Anderson looks straight at Scott and answers in unequivocal terms.

"Sir, he's up to no good. He's definitely involved in some plan or other. Let me first give you my take on Oswald."

"Go ahead, Chuck—I value your assessment. Shoot."

"Chief, let's go back to his Moscow days, his Soviet citizenship phase, and all that we know about his antecedents."

"Smart, very smart, Chuck. Go on."

"We have little or no data on his time in Moscow, other than the obvious facts of his citizenship change and our embassy's diplomatic reports, and the fact is that our people did not see him then as a subject for surveillance resources. Just a misguided former marine with an agenda. We received no reports on his political disposition, any adherence to Marxist-Leninist ideology or love of the Khrushchev government or the Russian people. In a nutshell, nada."

Anderson swallows some water and continues.

"So what is really going on here? He apparently becomes disenchanted with the Soviet Union, leaves, and comes here, but—and here's the *but*—in spite of so-called disenchantment, he's openly visiting and clearly working something or other with both the Soviets and the Cubans. What? We don't know. We need to find out rapidly, because if they're plotting some kind of comeback after last year's earth-shattering event with the missile crisis, then we could be in for a big surprise, and Washington needs to know."

"Agreed, Chuck, no question, we have to find out quickly. What do you need?"

"Well, first off, we need better listening and intercept equipment, and soonest. I'll let Holly spell out the request."

Holly Meacham is a very accomplished MIT electrical engineering graduate and Station Chief Winston Scott's go-to person for all things technical and for any kind of surveillance equipment.

"Sir, I've put in an urgent request for close-in listening equipment for use in the local restaurants where Oswald and his cohorts hang out, the latest that we have, which the team can use in situ to record their conversations. I also want to bug Oswald's hotel room, so we're figuring out how to do that. Chuck and the guys have a way in there, with staff at the hotel that we have paid. We can slip in during room-cleaning time and install. We're on top of that, but the other request to headquarters needs an urgent request update from you, sir."

"Got it. Draft me the message soonest, Holly, and we'll have it off to DC by midmorning, please."

"Count it as done, sir," says Holly.

"Back to Oswald's motivation, his associations, and his modus operandi. What do any of you think about Oswald's apparent volte-face? What do you really think is going on here?"

Chuck takes the lead.

"Chief, we've been analyzing this to death. There are clearly unexplained contradictions. His behavior is not at all consistent—in fact it's downright bewildering—but here's our best take. In a nutshell, Oswald has not turned against his Soviet predilections. He's clearly doing something with them and the Cubans. All things to all men. Now here's the rub. The Russians back in Moscow have gone out of their way to subtly tell us that Oswald is a no-gooder, not one of them, and he's, to put it crudely, 'a little wacko. Unbalanced—you can have him back; we don't need him here.' That's the line that they're peddling in Moscow about Lee Harvey Oswald. 'Take him back. He's yours.'"

"And what do you think of all this?"

"Well, Chief, it's very clear that this could well be a KGB subterfuge where instead of dissociating himself from Mother Russia, he heads straight for Mexico and into the arms of the KGB and the Cubans—people who are both joined at the hip and our mortal enemies. In other words, Oswald and the KGB are playing a game."

"So who's pulling his chain? Their local KGB head who we know all about, the Cubans, a joint Soviet-Cuban operation, what?"

"Most likely a combined Soviet-Cuban operation, and Oswald is now their asset."

"To do what? What's your best assessment?" asks Scott.

"That's why we need close-in surveillance. We don't have any source that's likely to know what's going on. None of our Mexican agents or locals who are working inside both embassies have access inside the inner sanctum of the KGB and the GRU. We all know who most of them are, but that's about it. What they have planned for Oswald is a mystery. We have to find out soonest."

"And Moscow's role? Is this coming from the top?"

"Great question, sir. Our best estimate is yes. Why would the KGB here in Mexico City be harmonizing with their Cuban friends and with Oswald? This had to start in Moscow. It has to be a plan. The Moscow line about Oswald's mental state is a subterfuge. They want us to think he's an outcast, no good to them, a liability, we can have him back."

"OK, I've got it. We have to find out ASAP what they're up to. Clearly no good. Let's intensify the surveillance and work to get the telephone operators in his hotel to record his telephone conversations. Pay them whatever they want. You have my approval here and now. Go do it."

"And his mail, if any?" asks Chuck.

"His mail too. Get the people or right person in the mail room on board. If he's receiving mail, we need to know from whom, what, and why. Whatever it takes, do it pronto."

"And the NSA, boss, can they help?"

"I've a call with Angleton later this morning about that, and I'll also talk with the attachés at their meeting this afternoon. If the Soviets are smart, which they are, they won't be transmitting any of their plans in the ether, however well encrypted. This will all be very closely held, totally sub rosa, by just a few with a need to know. Courier-pouch stuff, hand-carried backward and forward by their hoods in the KGB station."

"Are any of our other stations picking up snippets about what may be transpiring here in Mexico City?" asks Holly Meacham.

"Not so far, or at least nothing that headquarters is sharing with us. I'll go into all that with Angleton when we talk."

The meeting adjourns.

Chief of Station Scott is a very worried man. Something is afoot, and it isn't good. Oswald didn't simply just appear out of the blue in Mexico City and start cavorting with the KGB and the Cubans. Nothing is by accident, he surmises.

Scott sits back, alone in his office; he sips his coffee and reflects on a deep concern that has troubled him since the Bay of Pigs fiasco and the Cuban Missile Crisis.

He's heard reliable agency rumors via his closest associates, whom he goes way back with for decades, that the innermost closely guarded workings at Langley, outside the normal Directorate of Operations mainstream work, are seeking to foment trouble for Fidel Castro with the CONUS-based Cuban dissident opposition and people who are associated with the more right-wing opponents of the White House's now conciliatory approach to both Castro and Moscow. The latter is disturbing some within the political-military establishment.

Scott leans back, and a huge fear comes over him.

"What if the Soviets are smart and cunning enough to exploit internal US dissension regarding Cuba and Cuban-Soviet relations, plans, and operations?" Scott thinks aloud.

The Soviets are smart enough to know that President Kennedy won the election by a tiny margin, thinks Scott. He has many opponents, and the opposition creates an environment for sowing discord and playing two games at once: one that supports Fidel Castro to the hilt and another in parallel that undermines American policy by playing to the very faction that opposes Castro—the most evil and diabolical scenario.

His secretary enters and reminds him that it's ten minutes to go to his call with James Jesus Angleton at CIA headquarters in Langley, Virginia.

Scott mutters to himself as he opens the file that he wishes to discuss with Angleton: "A horse of a different color. No, a horse of a very, very different color. This man is a serious threat, and whoever is pulling this puppet's strings is even more so."

Lee Harvey Oswald is now top of the CIA's Mexico City station chief's agenda.

"I need more coffee, please," Scott calls to his secretary on the intercom.

He knows that any call with Angleton will not be easy.

CHAPTER 17
PRELUDE TO TRAGEDY

Angleton's secure phone rings.

"Angleton here. Oh, spot on time, Winston. How are you, and what's the latest in Mexico City? I've been closely following your messages."

Angleton pauses and lets Chief of Station Scott proceed.

"We're all fine down here. Working our proverbial tails off, and I'm a little stretched because of the surveillance demands. Could do with a few more bodies, but we'll cope; we have to. I'll be brief, boss, and give you all the salient points that the key staff here and I are most concerned about and what I'd like headquarters to do to help us. Not too demanding, but very necessary."

"Go ahead, Winston. I'm all ears, and I have just seen the urgent request your office sent regarding surveillance equipment. Not a problem. I've already signed off on it. We'll have it to you pronto. Go ahead."

"In three words, 'Lee Harvey Oswald.' He's our key target right now."

"Tell me about him. I've had the FBI meddling in our business, and they want more from us than my boss and I want to disclose. But let me hear what you've got to say about him."

"I think the bureau and state know what he's up to regarding visa applications. That's all in the paper chain, and it's easy to see what might be going on in this man's quite extraordinary mind. His motivation, goals, and Soviet-Cuban connections worry us—a lot."

"Go on, Winston. Yes, the FBI is fully in the picture about his apparent visa applications. The question is, What's behind it all? Who's pulling his chains? Moscow? Havana? Both? And possible connections with the people we know here in the Southwest and people that DD for plans, my boss, Richard Helms, has in his sights."

"Tell me more about all that, in case we can piece the puzzle together," says Scott.

"No, not right now. I want to hear more about what you have and your best assessment. Oswald is a threat but also perhaps an asset."

That last statement sends a shiver down Winston Scott's spine: "But also perhaps an asset."

What does Angleton mean by that? "Does he know something that I don't that would help my team figure out Oswald's objectives, likely modus operandi, and what he's up to with both the Soviets and the Cubans, separately or together?" These thoughts flash through Scott's astute mind.

Winston Scott pauses. His mind is going a thousand miles an hour.

"Are you still there, Winston?"

"Yes, I'm here, thinking. We have multiple options, sir, and none of them are dead certs: purely hypotheses at this stage, unless we can break into his conversations with his Soviet and Cuban contacts. His visits worry us, given his background. Our dilemma is simple. Who is he really working for and with? Or is he a misguided former marine who has totally lost his way in life? The latter seems very improbable, given his quite deliberate and planned exodus from the United States to Moscow, then a turnaround with the Soviets, who claim he's unstable and they don't like him or need him. None of this fits in with his return to the United States or now his comings and goings between the Soviet and Cuban embassies. His objectives? Well, the best we can tell is that others are pulling his strings. He's a puppet. The question is, Who really are his puppet masters, and what strings are they really pulling and why? What do 'they' want from Oswald?"

"Go on, Winston. This is good, very good. So what do you really think?"

"Well, he could be part of the most nefarious deception we've seen in a long time from our friends on Lubyanka Street in Moscow. They disown him, he returns to the United States, and then he comes here to Mexico City and proceeds to go to both the Soviet and Cuban embassies, ostensibly to obtain a Cuban visa. So why the Soviets? There's something that's going on between the Cubans and Moscow, with him in the middle. Now, here's the part that troubles my people and is in the realm of total speculation because we simply don't have any intercepted data, zero communications, and no one close enough to any of these players to give the game away."

"Your usual assets have nothing, then?" asks Angleton.

"Zero. We have a well-established group of people whom we've had on the payroll for a long time, reliable, honest, and tell us all that they know, but—and here's the *but*—none of them know what goes on when Oswald enters either of these two embassies. He seems to vanish from the usual Mexican clerks and admin people that we pay. His visa things are most likely a total subterfuge for other reasons, an excuse for his visits."

"So where is this all going, in your best judgment?"

"Most likely a move that's clearly aimed at an anti-Kennedy program that both Castro and Moscow together have cooked up. Castro has never got over our failure at the Bay of Pigs, and Moscow sees the post–missile crisis period now as a time to sow dissent and disaffection in the United States, given the delicate situation that the president faces regarding the vocal and active anti-Castro faction, plus the more militarist activists who are working to undermine Kennedy's policy to work out a modus vivendi with Moscow. Then you add the situation evolving in Vietnam to this equation, and one can rapidly see that the KGB will be seeking to find every means to undermine Kennedy internally while supporting its Cuban ally, Fidel Castro. In a nutshell, boss, it's a recipe for disaster if the complexity of internal US politics mixes with the disaffected anti-Cuban faction and the likes of a small cog called Lee Harvey Oswald, who could easily become the unwitting tool of any of these elements. Boss, a scary scenario."

Scott pauses.

Angleton chimes in.

"Winston, I want you to keep all this closely held. J. Edgar Hoover is poking his nose into our business, and my leadership, Dick Helms, wants the FBI out of our bailiwick. Don't connect with the FBI if they contact you or want to know what we're doing apropos Oswald and others. It's none of their business, plus we have other interests that the director wants kept extremely tight: so tight that only the key operators are in the know."

"And the Hill and the White House?"

"Not involved, Winston. Not in the know. Hoover and his boys will spill the beans all over town if they get a sniff of what we're trying to do regarding Castro and his Soviet controllers. The anti-Castro faction here in the United States and the powerful military lobby that abhors the president's policies are a factor. I'll say no more. I've said too much as it is. Forget what I just told you, Winston."

"Yes, sir. Got it. Meanwhile, any further specific instructions?"

"No, keep up the good work. Let's hope the communications equipment we're sending down pays dividends. Try to establish who the Soviet handlers are. Photos will help a lot."

"Do you have anything further for me?" asks Scott. "New insights at your end?"

"Well, I'll be in Israel shortly, and I'll try to see if my friends have anything useful."

"Maybe not a good time to raise this," interjects Scott, "but is there anything coming out of Philby's defection? Did he have his fingers in the Cuban pie? Maybe Philby knew what his handlers were up to with Oswald and the nature of their game plan?"

There is a pregnant pause. Angleton is breathless. If anyone had been in the room with him, they would have observed a deathly pallor overcome him and a new level of stress.

"Since his defection the British have gone cold. They're in shock. The political blowback is enormous. The guy they sent out there to interrogate and bring him back failed miserably. MI6 agent Nicholas Elliott screwed up beyond recognition. The top leadership here even thinks that it was possibly deliberate, to save MI6 the pain of a trial and the total public exposure of what's transpired since the 1930s."

"You mean a cover-up by another name? Is that what you're saying, boss?"

"In a word, yes. Keep this close. The agency is watching the Brits very closely. MI6 is in deep trouble. If I get anything from my British and Mossad sources, then I will let you know."

"OK. Thank you. Much appreciated."

"Well, I have to break off. The DD for plans wants to see me, and I'll report on what we've discussed. Helms will want to know what you've found.

Keep up the good work. Let me know as soon as you pick up anything that looks relevant and different from what we know, or rather don't know."

"Yes, sir, got it."

"Out here. Good luck, Winston. Keep up the good work."

"Yes, sir. Out here."

As Angleton collects his thoughts and papers for his meeting with Richard Helms, his mind can think of only two things.

Harold Kim Philby and Lee Harvey Oswald.

The date was propitious. Lee Harvey Oswald was in Mexico City as Angleton headed to the suite of the deputy director for plans. Between September 27 and October 2, 1963, the CIA station chief and his very able staff had done their best to keep tabs on Oswald and ascertain his motivation, associations, and likely goals over and beyond what the FBI knew to be his ostensible goal of obtaining a visa to visit Cuba.

As Angleton greeted Helms's secretary, he was promptly told that Helms was engaged in a secure call and would be a few minutes late for their meeting.

Angleton sat down, accepted coffee, and began to cogitate on his latest interaction with Chief of Station Scott.

Little did Angleton know then, nor could he even predict, the likely career end and death of Scott in April 1971. He would be the chief of station in Mexico City until 1969, having been first appointed there in 1956—an extraordinarily lengthy period of service in a single location. Scott was a very able man, recruited into the Office of Strategic Services (OSS) from the FBI in 1943.

What Angleton could not anticipate as he sat there musing about Oswald, Station Chief Scott, and the latter's plans to intercept Oswald's communications was that years later, the CIA would seize, after Scott's death, his personal papers and an audiotape recording of Lee Harvey Oswald, and worse still, the manuscript of his memoirs that he had intended to publish and had planned to discuss with Richard Helms, who was now CIA director. He died two days before this planned meeting. Much later, in the 1980s, the manuscript was returned to Scott's son, but—and this is a major *but*—with everything removed after 1947, the year the CIA was established. Scott's son would subsequently bring a lawsuit against the CIA, and some of the missing chapters from his manuscript were returned. Why, then, did the CIA do this? What was so vital?

As the buzzer went off on Helms's secretary's desk to let her know that his call was completed and Angleton could enter, Angleton stood and stretched and grasped his folder with its top secret code word markings.

Angleton entered the lion's den.

Would his head be in the lion's mouth, or was he part of the pride?

"Sit down, James, please. We need to chat. I have one urgent matter to discuss with you, and it's all related to our man in Mexico City and your work with him and our team there."

"I'm all ears, Richard." Angleton felt sufficiently comfortable, having built a personal rapport with Helms, that he could call him by his first name.

"Hoover and his people are all over us about this man Lee Harvey Oswald and what he's likely up to in Mexico City. They're aware of his visits to the Cuban and Soviet embassies and possible visa application to enter Cuba. I'm sure that you're all up to speed on this via Scott, correct?"

"Yes, sir, indeed, very much so. Watching it all very closely. We sent him some special communications intercept equipment."

"I'm aware. I saw all that. I think he'll get something of value, and I need to know immediately. If you hear from him on that score in particular, tell me immediately. Doesn't matter where I am or the time. OK?"

"Yes, sir. Got it. Will do."

"Now let's talk about Hoover and our very secure internal operations."

Angleton winced slightly. Was this to be a further revelation beyond what he was familiar with? Something more than the internal US counter-intelligence operations he was running? It was all sub rosa and all without congressional knowledge or, therefore, approval; it was at best highly inappropriate and at worst illegal, trespassing on FBI turf without Hoover's knowledge or consent.

Was the White House knowledgeable? Angleton knew that the answer was a firm negative, confirmed again by Helms's next words, which verged on expletives.

"Goddamn Kennedy and his lawyer brother have never got over the Bay of Pigs fiasco, James. I think they both hate us and don't trust us. We redeemed ourselves somewhat with the U-2 flights over Cuba last year, but Jack Kennedy has it in for us, and his brother is meddling from the legal side."

"Is it affecting our internal things? What we're doing in the Southwest with our operatives?"

Angleton now trespassed into a most sensitive arena of which he was already knowledgeable.

They both knew that after the Bay of Pigs, the agency had tried to regroup in its anti-Castro and anti-Cuba stance and operations. How could they get back? What to do next after such a disastrous and humiliating defeat, watched by the whole world?

Both men also knew one other incredibly sensitive fact: that Angleton was the instrument for implementation as head of CIA counterintelligence.

"James, you did a tremendous job back in fifty-six with your Israeli connections over Khrushchev's address to the Soviet Communist Party in their Great Hall in Moscow. Allen Dulles never forgot what you did. That piece of intelligence from Amos Manor in Shin Bet was dynamite. Not only was David Ben-Gurion ecstatic, but just about anyone who's worth a damn here in Washington also realized what it meant. George Kennan and those Washington Soviet policy gurus salivated. Now we have a problem and challenges of a different color."

Angleton shuffled in his chair. What was Helms going to say next? His instincts told him that after his negative references to the White House and the FBI, what was coming next was going to be about Angleton's highly secret clandestine operations inside the United States, and these were not classical counterintelligence operations against, for example, the KGB and the GRU and American citizens and other internal US surrogates who were being entrapped by the Soviets and other Warsaw Pact spy agencies to give up secrets. This was over and beyond all that. He and Helms knew only too well that all these types of operations were legally and constitutionally the sole preserve of the FBI, not the CIA. All material and evidence that the CIA might accumulate in such cases should be both shared with the

FBI and also handed over to them for internal US counterintelligence and, where and when necessary, the arrest and prosecution of wrongdoers.

Not so. Helms and Angleton were treading on very thin ice. They were not just transgressing constitutional niceties and well-established norms between the CIA and FBI; they were, in essence, breaking the law.

Angleton's predictions came true.

Helms opened up.

"James, since April 1961, after the Bay of Pigs disaster, we've been on the defensive, keeping our heads down and staying clear of Kennedy's obsessions: to seek compromise with the Soviets and tone down the situation with Castro. None of us go along with any of this. He beat Nixon by the very narrowest of margins. We've been pretty effective at keeping things under control and staying low while still achieving our operational objectives."

Angleton knew exactly to what he was referring and commented in a slightly obsequious way, "Fully agree, boss—the Kennedy brothers are a challenge to our national security, cozying up to the Soviets after the missile crisis and now pandering to the Cubans."

"Yea, verily to all that, James."

Just as Helms was about to tell Angleton what was really on his mind, his buzzer rang.

"Mr. Helms, a special report has just arrived from Mexico City, signed by the deputy, Allan White, and there's a highly classified intercept of a man called Oswald that communications is transferring to you in the inner SCIF."

"Thank you."

"Wow, then Winston Scott and his people have really been on the ball, acted pretty quickly while Oswald was still in Mexico City," said Angleton.

"Looks like it. We'll go next door in a moment, once the communications center sends it to me. Meanwhile, let me tell you what I want you to do with our special southwest enclave and how we might use it. Kennedy says that we let him down with the Bay of Pigs; well, I'm hoping that we can pull a few irons out of the fire that will please our worthy president at last."

"We're growing every week in the Texas and New Orleans groups," commented Angleton.

"Good, very good, just what I want to hear, and I'm due to brief the director tomorrow morning on who's who and what's what in the Southwest and how this ties in with our anti-Castro operations."

Helms was referring to CIA director John Alexander McCone (1902–1991), who was director in the years 1961–1965. After the Bay of Pigs invasion, President Kennedy forced the resignation of CIA director Allen Dulles and other key staff. McCone had replaced Dulles on November 29, 1961. President Kennedy's brother, Robert, the attorney general, had a say in McCone's selection.

"Operation Mongoose is well ahead, at least from what I can see," said Helms. He was referring to a highly secret campaign against Castro in Cuba. "I'll be interested to see what White and his people have come up with regarding Oswald. He's part of our plan, an ideal anti-Castro operator who can play both roles, for and against. We've come a long way in training Cuban insurgents against Castro, and the help of our US-based Cuban dissidents plus our key people in New Orleans—"

"Yes, sir," interrupted Angleton. "All the key people are up to speed, particularly our people in New Orleans."

"Good, good, that's what I wanted to hear. My one concern is this, and I want your candid assessment. We cannot afford another failure. We're dealing with a fairly nefarious group. There's possible homosexual connotations with one or two, or that's what I think I'm reading. I want to ensure that we stay well clear of local law enforcement, and we certainly don't want the FBI field office down there meddling. Our covert people will need protection. Make it happen, James; whatever else, bury these people however you need to so they never come to the surface."

"I have, sir. We've got multiple covers. No one will be able to figure out who's who, and I've gone to extraordinary lengths to keep the agency's fingerprints away from everything. No one can associate us with any of the people that we're running."

"Excellent, excellent work, James, just what I wanted to hear. The director will be apoplectic if anything goes off the rails and the FBI and the media get into any of this. Kennedy will have our guts for garters, and it will be the end of all of us."

"It won't happen, sir, rest assured. No fingerprints. Our people involved are the best of the best. You know who's at the forefront. I have every confidence in them."

"OK, I'm reassured. Let's go see next door what White's people have come up with on Mr. Lee Harvey Oswald. He's an interesting character, to put it mildly, and while we're in there looking at the product, tell me about how he fits in, with his background and what we're doing with him. I need to know. The FBI, and Hoover, will be all over us if they think that we're playing games with a former Soviet defector, marine sniper, and all the other things we know about this man. I saw that the FBI is up to speed on his visa application down in Mexico City. What else they've come up with I am going to be intrigued to see."

"You bet, sir. I'm ready when you are," said Angleton.

The two men retreated into the inner SCIF behind Helms's large desk, secured the door, and that was that.

New Orleans district attorney Jim Garrison later prosecuted Clay Shaw on the charge that Shaw and a group of anti-Cuban activists, including David Ferrie and Guy Banister, had been involved in a conspiracy with certain key classified elements of the CIA in President Kennedy's assassination. Garrison arrested Shaw on March 1, 1967. District Attorney Garrison believed that Shaw was the man named as "Clay Bertrand" in the Warren Commission Report into the assassination of President Kennedy. Garrison claimed that Shaw used this name as an alias in New Orleans gay society. The trial took place in January and February 1969. Insurance salesman Perry Russo testified that he had attended a party at the apartment of anti-Castro activist David Ferrie. Russo claimed that Oswald, Ferrie, and "Clay Bertrand" discussed assassinating Kennedy. He claimed that the conversation of these three men included plans for the "triangulation of crossfire" and alibis for the participants. All of this was challenged as unreliable. On March 1, 1969, Shaw was acquitted less than one hour after the judge sent the case to the jury. Shaw fervently denied all the allegations. Shaw died of metastatic lung cancer in August 1974, at the age of sixty-one. He was a heavy smoker. In 1979 Richard Helms, by then the former director of the CIA, testified under oath that Shaw had been a part-time CIA contact and that this was not at all unusual for typical CIA business-type contacts.

What Helms and Angleton saw and heard remains, at the time of this writing in November 2021, unknown. The material that was sent by Chief of Station Scott to CIA headquarters has not seen the light of day, even though Scott's family brought legal action to have his papers and materials released to the public. President Joe Biden has indicated that he wants all material that remains classified regarding President Kennedy's assassination to be released in one year's time, which will be the fall of 2022 if the schedule is maintained. The reason for withholding such material has been given as national security concerns. One can only speculate on what these might be. They may include special sources and methods; insights into US policies, and particularly the intelligence operations that support them, that even at this late date have some current relevance; and the need to prevent public outrage over various missteps and strategic errors by agencies of the US government, which may cause severe embarrassment and bring the United States and its agencies into both national and international disrepute. There may be other classified reasons, in addition. It is possible only to conjecture and speculate on the basis of the known facts.

One critical set of facts is on the record.

CIA director Richard Helms (1913–2002) began work with the Office of Strategic Services during World War II and was director from 1966 to 1973, deputy director from 1965 to 1966, and deputy director for plans from 1962 to 1965. In 1977, as a result of earlier covert operations in Chile, Helms became the only CIA director to be convicted of misleading Congress. He had also severely hampered the Senate Church Committee investigation into the CIA by ordering the destruction of all files relating to the CIA's mind control program. In federal court Helms pleaded nolo contendere that he "had not fully, completely, and accurately testified to Congress." He was convicted of this misdemeanor charge and received a two-year suspended sentence and a $2,000 fine. The trial judge, Barrington D. Parker, delivered scathing comments on Helms's conduct. James Jesus Angleton came out in total defense of Helms. After the federal court sentencing, Helms attended a gathering of CIA officers in Bethesda, Maryland, where he received a standing ovation. The gathering raised enough money from a private collection to pay Helms's $2,000 federal fine. He received other accolades, including an event with hundreds of guests at the Grand Ballroom of the Washington, DC, Hilton hotel. Later, in 1983, President Reagan awarded Helms the National Security Medal, and Helms was a proponent of William Casey becoming President Reagan's choice for CIA director. Casey subsequently served as DCI 1981–1987. Helms knew Casey from the OSS days in World War II. Helms was also presented with the Donovan Award, named after the famous founder of the OSS, William "Wild Bill" Donovan. Helms died in 2002 at the age of eighty-nine from multiple myeloma.

CHAPTER 18

"I'M JUST A PATSY" (LEE HARVEY OSWALD)

The tragic and earth-shattering event in Dealey Plaza, Dallas, Texas, on Friday, November 22, 1963—the assassination of the thirty-fifth president of the United States, John Fitzgerald Kennedy—remains ingrained in the annals of American and world history and, for those still alive who remember that day vividly, ingrained in the human psyche of all decent and compassionate people.

The man who the Warren Commission (named after its chairman, chief justice of the United States Earl Warren), in its 888-page final report, stated was the lone assassin was Lee Harvey Oswald.

Oswald made one hugely significant comment after the assassination and before he was fatally shot by Jack Ruby on November 23, 1963, while in police custody after being charged with the assassination of President Kennedy and the murder of Dallas police officer J. D. Tippit.

He said in a thoroughly convincing way, "I'm just a patsy."

Those few words say an awful lot.

The work of Jefferson Morley and John Newman has been acknowledged earlier. Their interview of Jane Roman, James Jesus Angleton's key staff person at the CIA, on November 2, 1994, is monumentally important. This interview was transcribed by Mary Bose of the *Washington Post* on November 7, 1994. Among many things, Jane Roman handled the incoming reports from Mexico City and what may be best described as "the Oswald file." She most likely saw everything that Angleton handled, unless he hid things from her for whatever reason.

Two key facts are evident. One, when Angleton testified after the Kennedy assassination, he committed perjury by not revealing that the CIA had data regarding Lee Harvey Oswald; and two, he never shared what was undoubtedly critical data regarding Lee Harvey Oswald with the FBI. The FBI was undoubtedly aware of Oswald's apparent desire to obtain a visa in Mexico City to visit Cuba, as well as of his movements in the United States. However, several critical aspects were neither shared nor subsequently disclosed.

"I'm just a patsy" implies one thing and one thing only.

Oswald clearly considered himself to have been used in the assassination by others. The implication is clear. Others were involved in the planning and execution of the president's assassination. The questions are who and why.

What was the fundamental motivation for the clearly well-planned assassination of John Fitzgerald Kennedy?

Oswald was a complex individual, though there seems to be no professional psychiatric evidence available to describe his mental state. Several of his key actions are well documented, and the Warren Commission report speaks for itself. However, that hugely dated report is undoubtedly not accurate, simply because Justice Warren and the members of the commission, through no fault of theirs, were totally unaware of key salient facts.

One of these facts is undoubtedly the role of the CIA and the information that James Jesus Angleton withheld: information whose omission amounted to perjury, insofar as he knew more about Oswald than he revealed. His failure to give full and complete disclosure during testimony was deliberate. There is no question about this. The later evidence collected by Jefferson Morley opens up Pandora's box. He had much information about Lee Harvey Oswald and those with whom he was associated in his files. Those files are critical evidence.

Richard Helms was without doubt an American patriot of the highest order and someone who truly believed that what he was doing was not just right in a moral sense but also vital for national security—and that certain data should not be made public knowledge. That data now needs to be in the public domain, and hopefully President Biden will order full disclosure at some point.

What might be hidden and why?

Oswald was by any standards not just a complex individual with a well-documented history in the marine corps, defection to the Soviet Union, apparent disillusionment with the Soviet Union, and return to the United States. None of this logically or automatically explains why he was there in Dealey Plaza on the fateful day in November 1963.

The very limited and not necessarily reliable evidence given out by the Soviet Union about Oswald—that he was of no consequence to them and in essence an unreliable and valueless asset for the likes of the KGB and the GRU—does bear analysis, but the facts are so scanty that speculation may be wildly inaccurate. The KGB files regarding Oswald may be the only true ways in which to validate the KGB's assessment of Oswald and his possible value to it as an agent.

It is perhaps much more accurate and reliable to examine Soviet policy goals and the likely intelligence and operations that may have flowed from KGB headquarters in Moscow. The Cuban Missile Crisis had been resolved not 100 percent in the favor of the United States. President Kennedy agreed as part of the settlement to deconstruct US missile sites in Turkey, a quid quo pro for the Soviets withdrawing the sites in Cuba. Kennedy wanted rapprochement with conditions with the Soviet Union while clearly building a positive and effective deterrence strategy.

Kennedy had a body of excellent political-military advisers, and he had shown cool, calm, and collected decision-making during the missile crisis. The rash, impetuous, and potentially horrendous impulses of the more belligerent members of the US military, such as General Curtis LeMay of the US Air Force, were discarded as not just bad policy but also highly dangerous inclinations for all concerned.

The Soviets undoubtedly recognized the political-military divergence in Washington, DC, between the Kennedy White House and other influential factions that were strongly anticommunist, anti-Soviet, and anti-Cuban, with a massive distain for Fidel Castro himself. One may argue that it was not in the Soviet interest to destabilize the Kennedy regime while at the same time continuing to support their client, Fidel Castro, in Cuba.

So where might Lee Harvey Oswald and the CIA fit into this complexity?

As we know from the findings of the Church Commission and CIA director Helms's federal prosecution and conviction, the CIA did not just withhold crucial information about its Chilean operations; there were, in addition, critical events occurring in the 1961–1963 period at the agency that Helms, with Angleton, had direct involvement in and control and direction over.

If he were alive today, Director Helms would undoubtedly argue in his own defense that having various ne'er-do-wells in the southeast United States providing information to the CIA was not unusual insofar as the agency regularly used civilian contacts, particularly in the business world, both to provide information and to perform special tasks.

The people that Helms and Angleton were using in the United States were undoubtedly not, in any shape or form, classic CIA operatives or agents, but they were being used. What for is the big question.

The answer is very clear with the benefit of hindsight and the testimony of Angleton's female assistant, referred to earlier. They may not have been paid agents, but they were very significant. The agency was still in the fight with Castro and had not forgotten its failures during the Bay of Pigs. Internal US Cuban dissidents and those other US citizens who supported them were therefore very useful for the agency in getting back at Castro and his cohorts.

The tragedy is clear.

In this mix of very dubious, indeed sleazy and untrustworthy people were also those who regarded the Kennedy presidency as a threat to the well-being of the United States: a misguided, inaccurate, and highly dangerous position.

Into this fray stepped Lee Harvey Oswald, back from the Soviet Union, traveling to Mexico City ostensibly to obtain a visa to travel to Cuba, and most significant of all, part of the anti-Cuba group of Americans who also abhorred John Fitzgerald Kennedy.

The tragic irony, and the reason successive presidents have been loath to sign off on the release of all the classified documents relating to President Kennedy's assassination, is likely to be this.

Here it is.

It is highly likely that Oswald was part of the group of Americans that the CIA was using in various informational and operational-planning modes in its anti-Cuba and anti-Castro plans and operations, which both Helms and Angleton had major responsibilities for and oversight over.

What the CIA undoubtedly did not know was the critical fact that several of the people in the US Southwest with whom they were engaged in these various nefarious anti-Cuba operations were also, in parallel, violently anti-Kennedy and vehemently against his administration's policies.

There is zero evidence that the CIA knew about or in any way condoned the other non-Cuban activities of these evildoers.

However, it is clear that successive US governments and presidents, in the interest of the United States' reputation in the eyes of the world, would not want it to be known that its key HUMINT intelligence agency had inadvertently and without any malice aforethought engaged with a group that included Lee Harvey Oswald in planning and carrying out the assassination of a great American president.

The latest and greatest computer programs will permit deep analysis of the events in Dealey Plaza.

The author is very much aware of the use of, for example, advanced Bayesian log-likelihood mathematical techniques for examining in the finest detail the issue, for example, of the number of shots fired in Dealey Plaza and their trajectories, time sequence, and origins. Such advanced modeling tools permit, for example, better determination of whether indeed Lee Harvey Oswald was the lone gunman that day or whether there were others and shots fired from alternate locations.

Bayesian techniques can help resolve these long-standing issues.

The tragedy of Dealey Plaza has direct similarities with 9/11.

What are these?

Key is the total failure of CIA-FBI direct cooperation and information sharing at all levels. Just as in the 9/11 scenario, the CIA failed to share vital intelligence with the FBI, and the FBI also failed to act on information from one of its field agents about flight training activities. The location of the terrorist group, particularly its leader, went unchecked. If the CIA had shared vital intelligence, the FBI could have intercepted communications and performed intensive surveillance of the flight trainees and the ringleader of the group, Mohamed Atta, the Egyptian hijacker-pilot of American Airlines

Flight 11, which he crashed into the North Tower of the World Trade Center as part of the coordinated attack. At thirty-three years of age, Atta was the oldest of the nineteen hijackers who took part in the attacks.

CIA-FBI data sharing and communications breakdowns had disastrous consequences in both 1963 and 2001.

In the middle of the 1963 debacle was James Jesus Angleton, the man who later would be systematically involved in the career destruction of key reputable, loyal, and highly capable CIA employees.

Angleton has much to answer for.

His relationship with Harold Kim Philby, like the events leading up to the tragedy in Dealey Plaza in November 1963, bears very close scrutiny.

CHAPTER 19

URINT:
"MORE THAN A FEELING IN THE WATER"

There are more sources and methods in the contemporary Five Eyes intelligence community than one can shake a stick at. The list is almost endless.

There is one type of intelligence collection and associated analysis that is not in any formal intelligence structure or acknowledged by the community.

This is URINT, a "feeling in the water." What is this? It sounds perhaps somewhat crude though hopefully not offensive.

Satellite data and communications intercept data tend to be highly reliable, though even those can be subject to deception. HUMINT may be notoriously unreliable, especially in the presence of "double agents." People like Oleg Antonovich Gordievsky, a highly reliable MI6 agent who was the KGB bureau chief in London and worked from 1974 to 1985 for British intelligence was one of a kind. Very few agents of his quality made themselves available to either the CIA or MI6. By contrast, Aldrich Ames at the CIA was a notorious spy for the KGB. At the time of his arrest, Ames had compromised more highly classified CIA assets in his counterintelligence role than any other officer in history—until Robert Hanssen's arrest seven years later in 2001. Hanssen worked for the FBI and, like Ames, was a counterintelligence specialist.

The intelligence process's key function is in the analysis of multisource data where all the various inputs from multiple intelligence sources and methods are aggregated and analyzed. Occasionally one single source may be golden, such as Gordievsky's material or a highly reliable satellite image

ANTHONY WELLS

or communications intercept. When these are assembled and analyzed, the intelligence community hopes for a reliable product that is then forwarded to the customer.

However, there are many occasions when the intelligence may not be reliable or, when aggregated, still presents uncertainty. In these situations, highly experienced intelligence specialists may resort to their best estimates based on decades of firsthand experience—this is their feeling in their water: URINT is the unprofessional rogue term. Often such estimates turn out to be highly reliable and are often supported, in current times, by the latest and greatest computational models using, for example, Bayesian mathematics and likelihood theory.

The intelligence data surrounding the exact and true nature of Harold Kim Philby and James Jesus Angleton's relationship is flimsy at best.

They had known each other during and since World War II and shared privately an inordinate amount of time together, exchanging intelligence. This we know.

What we do not know is whose side Angleton was really on.

Philby is a closed file, almost, albeit his relationship with Angleton remains a mystery. Much is known about Philby, and it is known that after his defection and a period of being watched in Moscow, he was fully accepted by the Soviet Union for what he truly was: a ruthless British traitor who had betrayed his country and Britain's allies.

The later Philby years in Beirut remain blurry in spite of more recent exposés about his defection in 1963. His meetings with Angleton during this period bear particular scrutiny. This was at a time when Angleton was consolidating his position and ruthless power as head of CIA counterintelligence and traveling to the Middle East, ostensibly to meet with his Mossad contacts. The years 1961–1963 were the years of the disastrous CIA Bay of Pigs operation, the Cuban Missile Crisis, and the assassination of President Kennedy.

Angleton was ruthless and powerful. He ruined many CIA careers as head of counterintelligence. Toward the end, before he was let go into retirement, many thought he verged on madness, seeking the hidden "mole" he was convinced was buried inside the inner sanctum of the CIA. Was he truly psychotic? Paranoid, perhaps? No one truly knows. What is known is that he abused his position to waste critical assets in what in retrospect were nothing more than counterintelligence subterfuges and wild-goose chases.

There is zero evidence that Angleton adhered at any time to some form of Marxist-Leninist ideology. Rather, almost the opposite. He could be complimented on his assiduous work in Italy in countering the emergence of an Italian communist party and its possible takeover of Italian politics. So there is little or no evidence to suggest that he had any affinity whatsoever with Soviet politics and its underlying ideology.

What, then, could possibly have motivated him in his relationship with Philby? How could he have been duped and deceived so successfully for so many years, from World War II onward, until the world learned of Philby's treachery? Angleton's tradecraft was not just out of bounds; it was also verging on the illicit in terms of his multiple private off-site meetings and exchanges with Philby over a protracted period.

There was the possible lure of loyalty to a country that he had admired greatly and spent time in as a young person: the United Kingdom. He had admired British intelligence's great triumphs during and shortly after World War II, particularly the exploits of Bletchley Park, British naval intelligence, the Double-Cross System, and the work of the British Special Operations Executive (SOE). "Wild Bill" Donovan admired British intelligence and modeled much of his newly formed Office of Strategic Services (OSS) on British naval intelligence and SOE. Angleton had his roots in OSS, so there was an inbred affinity for all things British.

So what does URINT conclude about Angleton and his relationship with the greatest British traitor of all time?

If all the data is assembled and analyzed with a fine-tooth comb, one may conclude that very indirectly Angleton was the unwitting agent of the KGB and GRU, since in his dealings with Philby, they collectively enhanced the Soviet intelligence database. That is probably an incontrovertible conclusion. He was, using the term that Lee Harvey Oswald made notorious, "a patsy," the tool of Harold Kim Philby, successfully manipulated for years.

Having said this, I should say there remain two very worrisome URINT factors that may change this otherwise unfortunate picture of a man who was allowed to rampage through the halls of the CIA for so long, unchecked and free to create counterintelligence mayhem.

Angleton was an educated man. He had shown his mettle in his youth and had what decades ago would have been termed "a good war." His later possible paranoia may have taken over. But what if this hypothesis is incorrect?

What if James Jesus Angleton created and conducted the worst counterintelligence operations ever known in any Western intelligence organization for specific reasons? He in effect not only destabilized CIA intelligence— he also directly interfered in British intelligence through his totally false and concocted claims. For one example, the head of Britain's MI5, Sir Roger Hollis, responsible for UK counterintelligence (he served with MI5 1938–1965 and was director general of MI5 1956–1965), was accused by Angleton of being a Soviet agent. For another, Angleton played deliberately and insidiously to the commentaries of British journalist Chapman Pincher and British intelligence officer Peter Wright; and worse still, he created the myth that British prime minister Harold Wilson had been recruited by the Soviets on much earlier visits to the USSR. He did the same in other allied countries. There was not one shred of serious evidence to support any of these false allegations. However, the effects were the same as inside the CIA. What were these?

He created instability, threw organizations into disarray, and slowed down intelligence processes while ruining careers. These outcomes are hugely serious. All this at a time when he had a deep-seated relationship with Britain's premier traitor.

What was the motivation if he was not of the same ilk as Philby and his Cambridge associates: a committed Marxist-Leninist?

Perhaps it was totally personal on both sides, Angleton's and Philby's. Each man was married and had children, and both had the ostensible public visages of married men. This did not preclude another kind of relationship.

Angleton was undoubtedly attracted to Philby. Perhaps infatuated at one level, indeed lured by Philby, seduced into the ways of the Cambridge traitors. Angleton could lie brazenly and successfully, as indeed he did to his country's Warren Commission. He, too, was capable of both deception and treachery of a different kind. It is undoubtedly a good URINT conclusion to state that the one side that Angleton undoubtedly was on was his own, enhanced and jaded by the following.

The classic interpretation of why people betray their countries and become spies for a foreign power has been based on three generic motivations. In legal terms the "mens rea" component of "actus reus, mens rea" denotes the thinking and intentions behind the act itself in criminal law. These are ideology, money, and sex, or some combination of the three.

From what is known about Philby, Burgess, and Maclean, there was a strong ideological motivation or component. In addition, it is suspected that they were also homosexual.

In an age when nonheterosexual sexual orientation was still not socially and legally accepted, it was a serious showstopper for homosexual people in their careers and personal lives. There was also a criminal element insofar as British laws condemned those found in homosexual situations. The tragic story of Alan Turing, the brilliant Bletchley Park code breaker, is a case in point that demonstrates the social and career consequences for an incredibly able man and great public servant who was accused of homosexual acts and was subject to humiliating therapies that today would be considered verging on torture. These involved chemical castration treatment. Turing died in 1954, sixteen days before his forty-second birthday, from cyanide poisoning. In 2009 the British prime minister Gordon Brown made an official public apology on behalf of the British government for "the appalling way he was treated." In 2013 Her Majesty Queen Elizabeth granted Turing a posthumous pardon.

In the environment in which Alan Turing lived, the Cambridge spies who were also homosexuals would have found themselves in extraordinary difficult circumstances and would have needed to avoid any form of governmental and legal action against them.

There is no current evidence to suggest that Angleton and Philby had a homosexual relationship. However, given the total circumstances regarding their relationship, it is neither unreasonable nor any way maliciously miscreant to suggest that they may perhaps have had a strong personal bond. How far this may have developed is totally speculative at this stage until other substantive hard evidence says otherwise. Perhaps the only way to establish this is in the classified files of both the CIA and MI6 that have not been released to the public.

Angleton may well have been exactly what many of his CIA colleagues considered him to be, namely an out-of-control head of counterintelligence with a paranoid conviction that the CIA was populated with a mole or moles. However, even the most paranoid person would have to produce positive evidence, and Angleton never did, and it is to the shame of the CIA leadership that the so-called watcher of those in the CIA, and particularly its clandestine Directorate of Operations, was not reviewed and called to account for his wanton attacks on reputable CIA employees and threats to their careers and futures.

The net effect of Angleton's actions was to undermine the efficiency and intelligence product from the CIA. He sowed, in essence, discord. It is also a matter of record that Angleton was a heavy drinker. He and Philby over-indulged. Whether both were actual alcoholics is unknown. The fact that they enjoyed each other's company with heavy drinking shows not just that they were professionally unconcerned about the effects of drinking on their duties but also that once together they simply did not care. Heavy alcohol consumption among close professional associates can lead to all manner of indiscretions. It is also a reflection on both CIA and MI6 oversight that these two men were not taken to task for their habits.

The hypothesis that Angleton was joined at the hip with Philby in supporting pro-Soviet plans, policies, and operations is a massive stretch. Given his whole career path, it is highly unlikely that he was ever recruited by Philby to work for the KGB.

What is very possible is that his special relationship with Philby was so subject to the blind loyalty factor that he indirectly aided Philby in treachery. The facts support this—I submit the single observation that Angleton gave Philby a lot of priceless information that ended up in Moscow before he presumably knew, or realized in early 1963, that Philby was indeed a Soviet agent all along.

Philby's defection to Moscow was not so much the "crowning glory" of Britain's worst spy—rather it was the nadir of Britain's counterintelligence capabilities working in tandem with Angleton's pervasive loyalty to and intoxication with Kim Philby.

EPILOGUE, BIOGRAPHIES, AND PHOTOGRAPHS OF PHILBY AND ANGLETON

There is much still to be revealed about the Philby-Angleton relationship. A full understanding of the events leading up to the assassination of President John Fitzgerald Kennedy is still not in any way complete. The fact that President Biden of the United States has declared that, in due course, remaining undisclosed classified intelligence material regarding the assassination will be made public knowledge speaks for itself.

Even today there are hidden files that will open up Pandora's box.

The reasons for nondisclosure have been discussed. Given the integrity of successive US presidents, it is clear that they may well have had very legitimate reasons for not disclosing all the known facts and particularly the intelligence aspects.

The roles Philby and Angleton in particular played in all this (other than what has been revealed in this book) remains to be seen. Both men were bad actors, with Philby being undoubtedly the worse of the two, a heinous traitor who cost lives and gave away critical secrets.

Their relationship has despicable aspects.

What is important today is the lessons that can be learned from reviewing their lives, their interactions, and the consequences of their relationship. The irony of this story is perhaps that James Jesus Angleton, as head of CIA counterintelligence, was able to operate for so long before being retired.

Oversight has hopefully been improved, and hopefully the vetting procedures associated with admitting personnel to the Five Eyes intelligence community have improved to obviate bad apples in the intelligence barrel.

The consequences of the Philby-Angleton connection were diabolically disastrous, and it behooves the leadership of the Five Eyes intelligence community to ensure that the likes of Philby and Angleton do not ever again slip though the net.

Philby and Angleton Biographies and Photos

Harold "Kim" Philby

Photo: Philby in 1955

	Harold Adrian Russell Philby
Born	1 January 1912 Ambala, Punjab, British India
Died	11 May 1988 (aged 76) Moscow, Russian SFSR, Soviet Union
Burial place	Kuntsevo Cemetery Ryabinovaya Ulitsa, Moscow
Nationality	British, Soviet
Alma mater	Westminster School Trinity College, Cambridge
Spouse(s)	• Litzi Friedmann • Aileen Furse • Eleanor Brewer • Rufina Ivanovna Pukhova
Parent(s)	• St John Philby • Dora Philby
Awards	Hero of the Soviet Union Order of Lenin Order of Friendship of Peoples
Espionage activity	
Country	United Kingdom
Allegiance	Soviet Union
Codename	Sonny, Stanley

Harold Adrian Russell "Kim" Philby (1 January 1912–11 May 1988) was a British intelligence officer and a double agent for the Soviet Union. In 1963 he was revealed to be a member of the Cambridge Five, a spy ring which had divulged British secrets to the Soviets during World War II and in the early stages of the Cold War. Of the five, Philby is believed to have been most successful in providing secret information to the Soviets.

Born in British India, Philby was educated at Westminster School and Trinity College, Cambridge. He was recruited by Soviet intelligence in 1934. After leaving Cambridge, Philby worked as a journalist, covering the Spanish Civil War and the Battle of France. In 1940 he began working for the United Kingdom's Secret Intelligence Service (SIS or MI6). By the end of the Second World War he had become a high-ranking member. In 1949 Philby was appointed first secretary to the British Embassy in Washington and served as chief British liaison with American intelligence agencies. During his career as an intelligence officer, he passed large amounts of intelligence to the Soviet Union, including a plot to subvert the communist regime of Albania.

Philby was also responsible for tipping off two other spies under suspicion of espionage, Donald Maclean and Guy Burgess, both of whom subsequently fled to Moscow in May 1951. The defections of Maclean and Burgess cast suspicion over Philby, resulting in his resignation from MI6 in July 1951. He was publicly exonerated in 1955, after which he resumed his career as both a journalist and a spy for SIS in Beirut, Lebanon. In January 1963, having finally been unmasked as a Soviet agent, Philby defected to Moscow, where he lived until his death in 1988.

Early life

Born in Ambala, Punjab, British India, Harold Adrian Russell Philby was the son of Dora Johnston and St John Philby, an author, Arabist and explorer St John was a member of the Indian Civil Service (ICS) and later a civil servant in Mesopotamia, and advisor to King Ibn Saud of Saudi Arabia.

Nicknamed "Kim" after the boy-spy in Rudyard Kipling's novel *Kim*, Philby attended Aldro preparatory school, an all-boys school located in Shackleford near Godalming in Surrey, England, United Kingdom. In his early teens, he spent some time with the Bedouin in the desert of Saudi Arabia. Following in the footsteps of his father, Philby continued to Westminster

School, which he left in 1928 at the age of 16. He won a scholarship to Trinity College, Cambridge, where he studied history and economics. He graduated in 1933 with a 2:1 degree in Economics.

At Cambridge, Philby showed his "leaning towards communism," in the words of his father St John, who went on to write: "The only serious question is whether Kim definitely intended to be disloyal to the government while in its service."

Upon Philby's graduation, Maurice Dobb, a fellow of King's College, Cambridge and tutor in Economics, introduced him to the World Federation for the Relief of the Victims of German fascism, an organization based in Paris which attempted to aid the people victimized by Nazi Germany and provide education on oppositions to fascism. The organization was one of several fronts operated by German communist Willi Münzenberg, a member of the Reichstag who had fled to France in 1933.

Early professional career

Vienna

In Vienna, working to aid refugees from Germany, Philby met Litzi Friedmann (born Alice Kohlmann), a young Austrian communist of Hungarian Jewish origins. Philby admired the strength of her political convictions and later recalled that at their first meeting:

Philby stated: "A frank and direct person, Litzi came out and asked me how much money I had. I replied £100, which I hoped would last me about a year in Vienna. She made some calculations and announced, "That will leave you an excess of £25. You can give that to the International Organization for Aid for Revolutionaries. We need it desperately." I liked her determination."

Philby acted as a courier between Vienna and Prague, paying for the train tickets out of his remaining £75 and using his British passport to evade suspicion. He also delivered clothes and money to refugees. Following the Austrofascist victory in the Austrian Civil War, Philby and Friedmann married in February 1934, enabling her to escape to the United Kingdom with him two months later.

It is possible that it was a Viennese-born friend of Friedmann's in London, Edith Tudor Hart, herself, at this time, a Soviet agent, who first approached Philby about the possibility of working for Soviet intelligence. In early 1934, Arnold Deutsch, a Soviet agent, was sent to University College London under the cover of a research appointment, but in reality had been assigned to recruit the brightest students from Britain's top universities. Philby had come to the Soviets' notice earlier that year in Vienna, where he had been involved in demonstrations against the government of Engelbert Dollfuss. In June 1934, Deutsch recruited him to the Soviet intelligence services, Philby later recalled:

Lizzy came home one evening and told me that she had arranged for me to meet a "man of decisive importance". I questioned her about it but she would give me no details. The rendezvous took place in Regents Park. The man described himself as Otto. I discovered much later from a photograph in MI5 files that the name he went by was Arnold Deutsch. I think that he was of Czech origin; about 5 ft 7in, stout, with blue eyes and light curly hair. Though a convinced Communist, he had a strong humanistic streak. He hated London, adored Paris, and spoke of it with deeply loving affection. He was a man of considerable cultural background."

Philby recommended to Deutsch several of his Cambridge contemporaries, including Donald Maclean, who at the time was working in the Foreign Office, as well as Guy Burgess, despite his personal reservations about Burgess's erratic personality.

London and Spain

In London, Philby began a career as a journalist. He took a job at a monthly magazine, the *World Review of Reviews*, for which he wrote a large number of articles and letters (sometimes under a variety of pseudonyms) and occasionally served as "acting editor."

Philby continued to live in the United Kingdom with his wife for several years. At this point, however, Philby and Friedmann separated. They remained friends for many years following their separation and divorced only in 1946, just following the end of World War II. When the Germans threatened to overrun Paris in 1940, where she was then living at this time,

Philby arranged for Friedmann's escape to Britain. In 1936 he began working at a failing trade magazine, the *Anglo-Russian Trade Gazette*, as editor. After the magazine's owner changed the paper's role to covering Anglo-German trade, Philby engaged in a concerted effort to make contact with Germans such as Joachim von Ribbentrop, at that time the German ambassador in London. He became a member of the Anglo-German Fellowship, an organization aiming at rebuilding and supporting a friendly relationship between Germany and the United Kingdom. The Anglo-German Fellowship, at this time, was supported both by the British and German governments, and Philby made many trips to Berlin.

In February 1937, Philby travelled to Seville, Spain, then embroiled in a bloody civil war triggered by the *coup d'état* of Falangist forces under General Francisco Franco against the democratic government of President Manuel Azaña. Philby worked at first as a freelance journalist; from May 1937, he served as a first-hand correspondent for *The Times*, reporting from the headquarters of the pro-Franco forces. He also began working for both Soviet and British intelligence, which usually consisted of posting letters in a crude code to a fictitious girlfriend, Mlle Dupont in Paris, for the Russians. He used a simpler system for MI6 delivering post at Hendaye, France, for the British Embassy in Paris. When visiting Paris after the war, he was shocked to discover that the address that he used for Mlle Dupont was that of the Soviet Embassy. His controller in Paris, the Latvian Ozolin-Haskins (code name Pierre), was shot in Moscow in 1937 during Joseph Stalin's Great Purge. His successor, Boris Bazarov, suffered the same fate two years later during the purges.

Both the British and the Soviets were interested in analyzing the combat performance of the new Messerschmitt Bf 109 fighter planes and Panzer I and Panzer II tanks deployed with Falangist forces in Spain. Philby told the British, after a direct question to Franco, that German troops would never be permitted to cross Spain to attack Gibraltar. Philby's Soviet controller at the time, Theodore Maly, reported in April 1937 to the NKVD that he had personally briefed Philby on the need "to discover the system of guarding Franco and his entourage". Maly was one of the Soviet Union's most powerful and influential illegal controllers and recruiters. With the goal of potentially arranging Franco's assassination, Philby was instructed to report on vulnerable points in Franco's security and recommend ways to gain access to him and his staff. However, such an act was never a real possibility; upon debriefing Philby in London on 24 May 1937, Maly wrote to the NKVD, "Though devoted and ready to sacrifice himself, [Philby] does not possess the physical courage and other qualities necessary for this [assassination] attempt."

In December 1937, during the Battle of Teruel, a Republican shell hit just in front of the car in which Philby was travelling with the correspondents Edward J. Neil of the Associated Press, Bradish Johnson of *Newsweek*, and Ernest Sheepshanks of Reuters. Johnson was killed outright, and Neil and Sheepshanks soon died of their injuries. Philby suffered only a minor head wound. As a result of this accident, Philby, who was well-liked by the Nationalist forces whose victories he trumpeted, was awarded the Red Cross of Military Merit by Franco on 2 March 1938. Philby found that the award proved helpful in obtaining access to fascist circles:

"Before then," he later wrote, "there had been a lot of criticism of British journalists from Franco officers who seemed to think that the British in general must be a lot of Communists because so many were fighting with the International Brigades. After I had been wounded and decorated by Franco himself, I became known as "the English-decorated-by-Franco", and all sorts of doors opened to me."

In 1938, Walter Krivitsky (born Samuel Ginsberg), a former GRU officer in Paris who had defected to France the previous year, travelled to the United States and published an account of his time in, "Stalin's secret service". He testified before the Dies Committee (later to become the House Un-American Activities Committee) regarding Soviet espionage within the US. In 1940 he was interviewed by MI5 officers in London, led by Jane Archer. Krivitsky claimed that two Soviet intelligence agents had penetrated the Foreign Office and that a third Soviet intelligence agent had worked as a journalist for a British newspaper during the civil war in Spain. No connection with Philby was made at the time, and Krivitsky was found shot in a Washington hotel room the following year.

Alexander Orlov (born Lev Feldbin; code-name Swede), Philby's controller in Madrid, who had once met him in Perpignan, France, also defected. To protect his family, still living in the USSR, Orlov said nothing about Philby, an agreement Stalin respected. On a short trip back from Spain, Philby tried to recruit Flora Solomon as a Soviet agent; she was the daughter of a Russian banker and gold dealer, a relative of the Rothschilds, and wife of a London stockbroker. At the same time, Burgess was trying to get her into MI6. But the *rezident* (Russian term for spymaster) in France, probably Pierre at this time, suggested to Moscow that he suspected Philby's motives. Solomon introduced Philby to the woman who would become Philby's second wife, Aileen Furse. Solomon went to work for the British retailer Marks & Spencer.

MI6 career

World War II

In July 1939, Philby returned to *The Times* office in London. When Britain declared war on Germany in September 1939, Philby's contact with his Soviet controllers was lost and Philby failed to attend the meetings that were necessary for his work. During the Phoney War from September 1939 until the Dunkirk evacuation, Philby worked as *The Times'* first-hand correspondent with the British Expeditionary Force headquarters. After being evacuated from Boulogne on 21 May, he returned to France in mid-June and began representing *The Daily Telegraph* in addition to *The Times*. He briefly reported from Cherbourg and Brest, sailing for Plymouth less than 24 hours before France surrendered to Germany in June 1940.

In 1940, on the recommendation of Burgess, Philby joined MI6's Section D, a secret organization charged with investigating how enemies might be attacked through non-military means. Philby and Burgess ran a training course for would-be saboteurs at Brickendonbury Manor in Hertfordshire. His time at Section D, however, was short-lived; the "tiny, ineffective, and slightly comic" section was soon absorbed by the Special Operations Executive (SOE) in the summer of 1940. Burgess was arrested in September for drunken driving and was subsequently fired, while Philby was appointed as an instructor on clandestine propaganda at the SOE's finishing school for agents at the Estate of Lord Montagu in Beaulieu, Hampshire.[31]

Philby's role as an instructor of sabotage agents again brought him to the attention of the Soviet Joint State Political Directorate (OGPU). This role allowed him to conduct sabotage and instruct agents on how to properly conduct sabotage. The new London *rezident*, Ivan Chichayev (code-name Vadim), re-established contact and asked for a list of names of British agents being trained to enter the Soviet Union. Philby replied that none had been sent and that none were undergoing training at that time. This statement was underlined twice in red and marked with two question marks, clearly indicating their confusion and questioning of this, by disbelieving staff at Moscow Central in the Lubyanka, according to Genrikh Borovik, who saw the telegrams much later in the KGB archives.

Philby provided Stalin with advance warning of Operation Barbarossa and of the Japanese intention to strike into Southeast Asia instead of attacking the Soviet Union as Hitler had urged. The first was ignored as a provocation, but the second, when this was confirmed by the Russo-German journalist and spy in Tokyo, Richard Sorge, contributed to Stalin's decision to begin transporting troops from the Far East in time for the counteroffensive around Moscow.

By September 1941, Philby began working for Section Five of MI6, a section responsible for offensive counter-intelligence. On the strength of his knowledge and experience of Franco's Spain, Philby was put in charge of the subsection which dealt with Spain and Portugal. This entailed responsibility for a network of undercover operatives in several cities such as Madrid, Lisbon, Gibraltar and Tangier. At this time, the German *Abwehr* was active in Spain, particularly around the British naval base of Gibraltar, which its agents hoped to watch with many cameras and radars to track Allied supply ships in the Western Mediterranean. Thanks to British counter-intelligence efforts, of which Philby's Iberian subsection formed a significant part, the project (code-named Bodden) never came to fruition.

During 1942–43, Philby's responsibilities were then expanded to include North Africa and Italy, and he was made the deputy head of Section Five under Major Felix Cowgill, an army officer seconded to SIS. In early 1944, as it became clear that the Soviet Union was likely to once more prove a significant adversary to Britain, SIS re-activated Section Nine, which dealt with anti-communist efforts. In late 1944 Philby, on instructions from his Soviet handler, maneuvered through the system successfully to replace Cowgill as head of Section Nine. Charles Arnold-Baker, an officer of German birth (born Wolfgang von Blumenthal) working for Richard Gatty in Belgium and later transferred to the Norwegian/Swedish border, voiced many suspicions of Philby and Philby's intentions but was ignored time and time again.

While working in Section Five, Philby became acquainted with James Jesus Angleton, the young American counter-intelligence officer working in liaison with SIS in London. Angleton later became Chief of the Central Intelligence Agency's (CIA) Counterintelligence Staff.

In late summer 1943, the SIS provided the GRU an official report on the activities of German agents in Bulgaria and Romania, soon to be invaded by the Soviet Union. The NKVD complained to Cecil Barclay, the SIS representative in Moscow, that information had been withheld. Barclay reported the complaint to London. Philby claimed to have overheard discussion of this by chance and sent a report to his controller. This turned out to be identical with Barclay's dispatch, convincing the NKVD that Philby had seen the full Barclay report. A similar lapse occurred with a report from the Imperial Japanese Embassy in Moscow sent to Tokyo. The NKVD received the same report from Richard Sorge but with an extra paragraph claiming that Hitler might seek a separate peace with the Soviet Union. These lapses by Philby aroused intense suspicion in Moscow.

Elena Modrzhinskaya at GUGB headquarters in Moscow assessed all material from the Cambridge Five. She noted that they produced an extraordinary wealth of information on German war plans but next to nothing on the repeated question of British penetration of Soviet intelligence in either London or Moscow. Philby had repeated his claim that there were no such agents. She asked, "Could the SIS really be such fools they failed to notice suitcase-loads of papers leaving the office? Could they have overlooked Philby's Communist wife?" Modrzhinskaya concluded that all were double agents, working essentially for the British.

A more serious incident occurred in August 1945, when Konstantin Volkov, an NKVD agent and vice-consul in Istanbul, requested political asylum in Britain for himself and his wife. For a large sum of money, Volkov offered the names of three Soviet agents inside Britain, two of whom worked in the Foreign Office and a third who worked in counter-espionage in London. Philby was given the task of dealing with Volkov by British intelligence. He warned the Soviets of the attempted defection and travelled personally to Istanbul – ostensibly to handle the matter on behalf of SIS but, in reality, to ensure that Volkov had been neutralized. By the time he arrived in Turkey, three weeks later, Volkov had been removed to Moscow.

The intervention of Philby in the affair and the subsequent capture of Volkov by the Soviets might have seriously compromised Philby's position. However, Volkov's defection had been discussed with the British Embassy in Ankara on telephones which turned out to have been tapped by Soviet intelligence. Additionally, Volkov had insisted that all written communications about him take place by bag rather than by telegraph, causing a delay in reaction that might plausibly have given the Soviets time to uncover his plans. Philby was thus able to evade blame and detection.

A month later Igor Gouzenko, a cipher clerk in Ottawa, took political asylum in Canada and gave the Royal Canadian Mounted Police names of agents operating within the British Empire that were known to him. When Jane Archer (who had interviewed Krivitsky) was appointed to Philby's section he moved her off investigatory work in case she became aware of his past. He later wrote, "she had got a tantalizing scrap of information about a young English journalist whom the Soviet intelligence had sent to Spain during the Civil War. And here she was plunked down in my midst!"

Philby, "employed in a Department of the Foreign Office", was awarded the Order of the British Empire in 1946.

Istanbul

In February 1947, Philby was appointed head of British intelligence for Turkey, and posted to Istanbul with his second wife, Aileen, and their family. His public position was that of First Secretary at the British Consulate; in reality, his intelligence work required overseeing British agents and working with the Turkish security services.

Philby planned to infiltrate five or six groups of émigrés into Soviet Armenia or Soviet Georgia. But efforts among the expatriate community in Paris produced just two recruits. Turkish intelligence took them to a border crossing into Georgia but soon afterwards shots were heard. Another effort was made using a Turkish gulet for a seaborne landing, but it never left port. He was implicated in a similar campaign in Albania. Colonel David Smiley, an aristocratic Guards officer who had helped Enver Hoxha and his Communist guerillas to liberate Albania, now prepared to remove Hoxha. He trained Albanian commandos, some of whom were former Nazi collaborators, in Libya or Malta. From 1947, they infiltrated the southern mountains to build support for former King Zog.

The first three missions, overland from Greece, were trouble-free. Larger numbers were landed by sea and air under Operation Valuable, which continued until 1951, increasingly under the influence of the newly formed CIA. Stewart Menzies, head of SIS, disliked the idea, which was promoted by former SOE men now in SIS. Most infiltrators were caught by the Sigurimi, the Albanian Security Service. Clearly there had been leaks and Philby was later suspected as one of the leakers. His own comment was, "I do not say that people were happy under the regime but the CIA underestimated the degree of control that the Authorities had over the country," Philby later wrote of his attitude towards the operation in Albania:

"The agents we sent into Albania were armed men intent on murder, sabotage and assassination. They knew the risks they were running. I was serving the interests of the Soviet Union and those interests required that these men were defeated. To the extent that I helped defeat them, even if it caused their deaths, I have no regrets."

Aileen Philby had suffered since childhood from psychological problems which caused her to inflict injuries upon herself. In 1948, troubled by the heavy drinking and frequent depressions that had become a feature of her husband's life in Istanbul, she experienced a breakdown of this nature, staging an accident and injecting herself with urine and insulin to cause skin disfigurations. She was sent to a clinic in Switzerland to recover. Upon her return to Istanbul in late 1948, she was badly burned in an incident with a charcoal stove and returned to Switzerland. Shortly afterward, Philby was moved to the job as Chief SIS representative in Washington, D.C., with his family.

Washington, D.C.

In September 1949, the Philbys arrived in the United States. Officially, his post was that of First Secretary to the British Embassy; in reality, he served as chief British intelligence representative in Washington. His office oversaw a large amount of urgent and top-secret communications between the United States and London. Philby was also responsible for liaising with the CIA and promoting "more aggressive Anglo-American intelligence operations". A leading figure within the CIA was James Jesus Angleton, with whom he once again found himself working closely. Angleton lunched with Philby at the very least once every week in Washington.

A serious threat to Philby's position came to light. During the summer of 1945, a Soviet cipher clerk had reused a one-time pad to transmit intelligence traffic. This mistake made it possible to break the normally impregnable code. Contained in the traffic (intercepted and decrypted as part of the Venona project) was information that documents had been sent to Moscow from the British Embassy in Washington. The intercepted messages revealed that the British Embassy source (identified as "Homer") travelled to New York City to meet his Soviet contact twice a week. Philby had been briefed on the situation shortly before reaching Washington in 1949; it was clear to Philby that the agent was Donald Maclean, who worked in the British Embassy at the time and whose wife, Melinda, lived in New York. Philby had to help discover the identity of "Homer", but also wished to protect Maclean.

In January 1950, on evidence provided by the Venona intercepts, Soviet atomic spy Klaus Fuchs was arrested. His arrest led to others: Harry Gold, a courier with whom Fuchs had worked, David Greenglass, and Julius and Ethel Rosenberg. The investigation into the British Embassy leak was still ongoing, and the stress of it was exacerbated by the arrival in Washington, in October 1950, of Guy Burgess, Philby's unstable and dangerously alcoholic fellow Soviet spy.

Burgess, who had been given a post as Second Secretary at the British Embassy, took up residence in the Philby family home and rapidly set about causing offence to all and sundry. Aileen Philby resented him and disliked his presence; Americans were offended by his "natural superciliousness" and "utter contempt for the whole pyramid of values, attitudes, and courtesies of the American way of life". J. Edgar Hoover complained that Burgess used British Embassy automobiles to avoid arrest when he cruised Washington in pursuit of homosexual encounters. His dissolution had a troubling effect on Philby; the morning after a particularly disastrous and drunken party, a guest returning to collect his car heard voices upstairs and found "Kim and Guy in the bedroom drinking champagne. They had already been down to the Embassy but being unable to work had come back."

Burgess's presence was problematic for Philby, yet it was potentially dangerous for Philby to leave him unsupervised. The situation in Washington was tense. From April 1950, Maclean had been the prime suspect in the investigation into the Embassy leak. Philby had undertaken to devise an escape plan which would warn Maclean, currently in England, of the intense suspicion he was under and arrange for him to flee. Burgess had to get to London to warn Maclean, who was under surveillance. In early May 1951, Burgess got three speeding tickets in a single day, then pleaded diplomatic immunity, causing an official complaint to be made to the British Ambassador. Burgess was sent back to England, where he met Maclean in his London club.

The SIS planned to interrogate Maclean on 28 May 1951. On 23 May, concerned that Maclean had not yet fled, Philby wired Burgess, ostensibly about his Lincoln convertible abandoned in the Embassy car park. "If he did not act at once it would be too late," the telegram read, "because [Philby] would send his car to the scrap heap. There was nothing more [he] could do." On 25 May, Burgess drove Maclean from his home at Tatsfield, Surrey to Southampton, where both boarded the steamship *Falaise* to France and then proceeded to Moscow.

London

Burgess had intended to aid Maclean in his escape, not accompany him in it. The "affair of the missing diplomats," as it was referred to before Burgess and Maclean surfaced in Moscow, attracted a great deal of public attention, and Burgess's disappearance, which identified him as complicit in Maclean's espionage, deeply compromised Philby's position. Under a cloud of suspicion raised by his highly visible and intimate association with Burgess, Philby returned to London. There, he underwent MI5 interrogation aimed at ascertaining whether he had acted as a "third man" in Burgess and Maclean's spy ring. In July 1951, he resigned from MI6, preempting his all-but-inevitable dismissal.

Even after Philby's departure from MI6, speculation regarding his possible Soviet affiliations continued. Interrogated repeatedly regarding his intelligence work and his connection with Burgess, he continued to deny that he had acted as a Soviet agent. From 1952, Philby struggled to find work as a journalist and eventually, in August 1954, accepting a position with a diplomatic newsletter called the *Fleet Street Letter*. Lacking access to material of value and out of touch with Soviet intelligence, he all but ceased to operate as a Soviet agent.

On 25 October 1955, following revelations in the *New York Times*, Labor MP Marcus Lipton used parliamentary privilege to ask Prime Minister Anthony Eden if he was determined, "to cover up at all costs the dubious third man activities of Mr. Harold Philby." This was reported in the British press, leading Philby to threaten legal action against Lipton if he repeated his accusations outside Parliament. Lipton later withdrew his comments. This retraction came about when Philby was officially cleared by Foreign Secretary Harold Macmillan on 7 November. The minister told the House of Commons, "I have no reason to conclude that Mr. Philby has at any time betrayed the interests of his country, or to identify him with the so-called 'Third Man', if indeed there was one." Following this, Philby gave a press conference in which, calmly, confidently, and without the stammer he had struggled with since childhood, he reiterated his innocence, declaring, "I have never been a communist."

Later life and defection

Beirut

After being exonerated, Philby was no longer employed by MI6 and Soviet intelligence lost all contact with him. In August, 1956 he was sent to Beirut as a Middle East correspondent for *The Observer* and *The Economist*. There, his journalism served as cover for renewed work for MI6.

In Lebanon, Philby at first lived in Mahalla Jamil, his father's large household located in the village of Ajaltoun, just outside Beirut. Following the departure of his father and stepbrothers for Saudi Arabia, Philby continued to live alone in Ajaltoun, but took a flat in Beirut after beginning an affair with Eleanor, the Seattle-born wife of *New York Times* correspondent Sam Pope Brewer. Following Aileen Philby's death in 1957 and Eleanor's subsequent divorce from Brewer, Philby and Eleanor were married in London in 1959 and set up house together in Beirut. From 1960, Philby's formerly marginal work as a journalist became more substantial and he frequently travelled throughout the Middle East, including Saudi Arabia, Egypt, Jordan, Kuwait and Yemen.

In 1961, Anatoliy Golitsyn, a major in the First Chief Directorate of the KGB, defected to the United States from his diplomatic post in Helsinki. Golitsyn offered the CIA revelations of Soviet agents within American and British intelligence services. Following his debriefing in the US, Golitsyn was sent to SIS for further questioning. The head of MI6, Dick White, only recently transferred from MI5, had suspected Philby as the "third man". Golitsyn proceeded to confirm White's suspicions about Philby's role. Nicholas Elliott, an MI6 officer recently stationed in Beirut, who was a friend of Philby's, and had previously believed in his innocence, was tasked with attempting to secure Philby's full confession.

It is unclear whether Philby had been alerted, but Eleanor noted that as 1962 wore on, expressions of tension in his life, "became worse and were reflected in bouts of deep depression and drinking". She recalled returning home to Beirut from a sight-seeing trip in Jordan to find Philby, "hopelessly drunk and incoherent with grief on the terrace of the flat," mourning the death of a little pet fox which had fallen from the balcony. When Nicholas

Elliott met Philby in late 1962, the first time since Golitsyn's defection, he found Philby too drunk to stand and with a bandaged head; he had fallen repeatedly and cracked his skull on a bathroom radiator, requiring stitches.

Philby told Elliott that he was, "half expecting", to see him. Elliott confronted him, saying, "I once looked up to you, Kim. My God, how I despise you now. I hope you've enough decency left to understand why". Prompted by Elliott's accusations, Philby confirmed the charges of espionage and described his intelligence activities on behalf of the Soviets. However, when Elliott asked him to sign a written statement, he hesitated and requested a delay in the interrogation. Another meeting was scheduled to take place in the last week of January. It has since been suggested that the whole confrontation with Elliott had been a charade to convince the KGB that Philby had to be brought back to Moscow, where he could serve as a British penetration agent of Moscow Center.

On the evening of 23 January 1963, Philby vanished from Beirut, failing to meet his wife for a dinner party at the home of Glencairn Balfour Paul, First Secretary at the British Embassy. The *Dolmatova*, a Soviet freighter bound for Odessa, had left Beirut that morning so abruptly that cargo was left scattered over the docks; Philby claimed that he left Beirut on board this ship. However, others maintain that he escaped through Syria, overland to Soviet Armenia and thence to Russia.

It was not until 1 Jul, 1963 that Philby's flight to Moscow was officially confirmed. On 30 July Soviet officials announced that they had granted him political asylum in the USSR, along with Soviet citizenship. When the news broke, MI6 came under criticism for failing to anticipate and block Philby's defection, though Elliott was to claim he could not have prevented Philby's flight. Journalist Ben Macintyre, author of several works on espionage, wrote in his 2014 book on Philby that MI6 might have left open the opportunity for Philby to flee to Moscow to avoid an embarrassing public trial. Philby himself thought this might have been the case, according to Macintyre.

Moscow
Upon his arrival in Moscow in January 1963, Philby discovered that he was not a colonel in the KGB, as he had been led to believe. He was paid 500

rubles a month (average soviet salary in 1960 was 80.6 rubles a month and 122 in 1970) and his family was not immediately able to join him in exile. Philby was under virtual house arrest, guarded, with all visitors screened by the KGB. It was ten years before he was given a minor role in the training of KGB recruits. Mikhail, his closest KGB contact, explained that this was to guard his safety, but later admitted that the real reason was the KGB's fear that Philby would return to London.

Secret files released to the National Archives in late 2020 indicated that the government had intentionally conducted a campaign to keep Kim Philby's spying confidential, "to minimize political embarrassment" and prevented the publication of his memoirs, according to a report by *The Guardian*. Nonetheless, the information was publicized in 1967 when Philby granted an interview to Murray Sayle of *The Times* in Moscow. Philby confirmed that he had worked for the KGB and that, "his purpose in life was to destroy imperialism".

Philby occupied himself by writing his memoirs, which were published in the UK in 1968 under the title *My Silent War*; it was not published in the Soviet Union until 1980. In the book, Philby says that his loyalties were always with the communists; he considered himself not to have been a double agent but, "a straight penetration agent working in the Soviet interest". Philby continued to read *The Times*, which was not generally available in the USSR, listened to the BBC World Service, and was an avid follower of cricket.

Philby's award of the Order of the British Empire was cancelled and annulled in 1965.Though Philby claimed publicly in January, 1988 that he did not regret his decisions and that he missed nothing about England except some friends, Colman's mustard, and Lea & Perrins Worcestershire sauce, his wife Rufina Ivanovna Pukhova later described Philby as, "disappointed in many ways, by what he found in Moscow. "He saw people suffering too much", but he consoled himself by arguing that, "the ideals were right but the way they were carried out was wrong. The fault lay with the people in charge", Pukhova said, "he was struck by disappointment, brought to tears. He said, "Why do old people live so badly here? After all, they won the war". Philby drank heavily and suffered from loneliness and depression;

according to Rufina, he had attempted suicide by slashing his wrists some time in the 1960s.

Philby found work in the early 1970s in the KGB's Active Measures Department churning out fabricated documents. Working from genuine unclassified and public CIA or US Department of State documents, Philby inserted "sinister" paragraphs regarding US plans. The KGB would stamp the documents, "Top Secret" and begin their circulation. For the Soviets, Philby was an invaluable asset, ensuring the correct use of idiomatic and diplomatic English phrases in their disinformation efforts.

Philby died of heart failure in Moscow in 1988. He was given a hero's funeral, and posthumously awarded numerous medals by the Soviets: Order of Lenin, Order of the Red Banner, Order of Friendship of Peoples, Order of the Great Patriotic War, Lenin Medal, Jubilee Medal, "Forty Years of Victory in the Great Patriotic War 1941–1945".

Motivation

In a 1981 lecture to the East German security service, Stasi, Philby attributed the failure of the British Secret Service to unmask him as due in great part to the British class system. It was inconceivable that one, "born into the ruling class of the British Empire" would be a traitor, to the amateurish and incompetent nature of the organization, and to so many in MI6 having so much to lose if he was proven to be a spy. He had the policy of never confessing, a document in his own handwriting was dismissed as a forgery. He said that at the time of his recruitment as a spy there were no prospects of his being useful; he was instructed to make his way into the Secret Service, which took years, starting with journalism and building up contacts in the "Establishment". He said that there was no discipline there; he made friends with the archivist, which enabled him for years to take secret documents home, many unrelated to his own work, and bring them back the next day; his handler took and photographed them overnight. When he was instructed to remove and replace his boss, Felix Cowgill, he asked if it was proposed, "to shoot him or something", but was told to use bureaucratic intrigue. He said, "It was a very dirty story, but after all our work does imply getting dirty hands from time to time but we do it for a cause that is not dirty in any way". Commenting on his sabotage of the operation to secretly send thousands of Albanian anti-communists into their Albania to overthrow the communist government, which led to many being killed, Philby rebutted that he helped prevent another World War.

Personal life

Memorial in Kuntsevo Cemetery, Moscow

In February 1934, Philby married Litzi Friedmann, an Austrian Jewish communist whom he had met in Vienna. They subsequently moved to Britain; however, as Philby assumed the role of a fascist sympathizer, they separated. Litzi lived in Paris before returning to London for the duration of the war; she ultimately settled in East Germany.

While working as a correspondent in Spain, Philby began an affair with Frances Doble, Lady Lindsay-Hogg, an actress and aristocratic divorcée who was an admirer of Franco and Hitler. They travelled together in Spain through August 1939.

In 1940 he began living with Aileen Furse in London. Their first three children, Josephine, John and Tommy Philby, were born between 1941 and 1944. In 1946, Philby finally arranged a formal divorce from Litzi. He and Aileen were married on 25 September 1946, while Aileen was pregnant with their fourth child, Miranda. Their fifth child, Harry George, was born in 1950. Aileen suffered from psychiatric problems, which grew more severe during the period of poverty and suspicion following the flight of Burgess and Maclean. She lived separately from Philby, settling with their children in Crowborough while he lived first in London and later in Beirut. Weakened by alcoholism and frequent sickness, she died of influenza in December 1957.

In 1956, Philby began an affair with Eleanor Brewer, the wife of *The New York Times* correspondent Sam Pope Brewer. Following Eleanor's divorce, the couple married in January 1959. After Philby defected to the Soviet Union in 1963, Eleanor visited him in Moscow. In November 1964, after a visit to the United States, she returned, intending to settle permanently. In her absence, Philby had begun an affair with Donald Maclean's wife,

Melinda. He and Eleanor divorced and she departed Moscow in May 1965. Melinda left Maclean and briefly lived with Philby in Moscow. In 1968 she returned to Maclean.

In 1971, Philby married Rufina Pukhova, a Russo-Polish woman twenty years his junior, with whom he lived until his death in 1988.

Fiction based on actual events

- *Philby, Burgess and Maclean*, a Granada TV drama written by Ian Curteis in 1977, covers the period of the late 1940s, when British intelligence investigated Maclean until 1955 when the British government cleared Philby because it did not have enough evidence to convict him.

- Philby has a key role in Mike Ripley's short story *Gold Sword* published in 'John Creasey's Crime Collection 1990' which was chosen as BBC Radio 4's Afternoon Story to mark the 50th anniversary of D-Day on 6 June 1994.

- *Cambridge Spies*, a 2003 four-part BBC drama, recounts the lives of Philby, Burgess, Blunt and Maclean from their Cambridge days in the 1930s through the defection of Burgess and Maclean in 1951. Philby is played by Toby Stephens.

- German author Barbara Honigmann's *Ein Kapitel aus meinem Leben* tells the history of Philby's first wife, Litzi, from the perspective of her daughter.

- Belgian comic authors Olivier Neuray and Valerie Lemaire wrote a series of three historical comics entitled "Les Cinq de Cambridge" involving Kim Philby. It was published by Casterman in 2015

Speculative fiction

- One of the earliest appearances of Philby as a character in fiction was in the 1974 *Gentleman Traitor* by Alan Williams, in which Philby goes back to working for British intelligence in the 1970s.

- In the 1980 British television film *Closing Ranks*, a false Soviet defector sent to sow confusion and distrust in British intelligence is unmasked and returned to the Soviet Union. In the final scene, it is revealed that the key information was provided by Philby in Moscow, where he is still working for British intelligence.

- In the 1981 Ted Allbeury novel *The Other Side of Silence*, an elderly Philby arouses suspicion when he states his desire to return to England.

- The 1984 Frederick Forsyth novel *The Fourth Protocol* features an elderly Philby's involvement in a plot to trigger a nuclear explosion in Britain. In the novel, Philby is a much more influential and connected figure in his Moscow exile than he apparently was in reality.

  - In the 1987 adaptation of the novel, also named *The Fourth Protocol*, Philby is portrayed by Michael Bilton. Even though he was still alive at the time of the film's release, he is executed by the KGB in the opening scene.

- In the 2000 *Doctor Who* novel *Endgame*, the Doctor travels to London in 1951 and matches wits with Philby and the rest of the Cambridge Five.

- The Tim Powers novel *Declare* (2001) is partly based on unexplained aspects of Philby's life, providing a supernatural context for his behavior.

- The Robert Littell novel *The Company* (2002) features Philby as a confidant of former CIA Counter-Intelligence chief James Angleton. The book was adapted for the 2007 TNT television three-part series *The Company*, produced by Ridley Scott, Tony Scott and John Calley; Philby is portrayed by Tom Hollander.

- Philby appears as one of the central antagonists in William F. Buckley Jr.'s 2004 novel *Last Call for Blackford Oakes*.

- The 2013 Jefferson Flanders novel *The North Building* explores the role of Philby in passing American military secrets to the Soviets during the Korean War.[102]

- Daniel Silva's 2018 book, *The Other Woman* is largely based on Philby's life mission

In alternative histories

- The 2003 novel *Fox at the Front* by Douglas Niles and Michael Dobson depicts Philby selling secrets to the Soviet Union during the alternate Battle of the Bulge where German Field Marshal Erwin Rommel turns on the Nazis and assists the Allies in capturing all of Berlin. Before he can sell the secret of the atomic bomb to the Soviet Union, he is discovered by the British and is killed by members of MI5 who stage his death as a heart attack.

- The 2005 John Birmingham novel *Designated Targets* features a cameo of Philby, under orders from Moscow to assist Otto Skorzeny's mission to assassinate Winston Churchill.

Fictional characters based on Philby

- The 1971 BBC television drama *Traitor* starred John Le Mesurier as Adrian Harris, a character loosely based on Kim Philby.

- John le Carré depicts a Philby-like upper-class traitor in the 1974 novel *Tinker Tailor Soldier Spy*. The novel has been adapted as a 1979 TV miniseries, a 2011 film, and radio dramatizations in 1988 and 2009. In real life, Philby had ended le Carré's intelligence officer career by betraying his British agent cover to the Russians.

- In the 1977 book *The Jigsaw Man* by Dorothea Bennett and the 1983 film adaption of it, *The Jigsaw Man*, "Sir Philip Kimberly" is a former head of the British Secret Service who defected to Russia, who is then given plastic surgery and sent back to Britain on a spy mission.

- Under the cover name of 'Mowgli' Philby appears in Duncan Kyle's World War II thriller *Black Camelot* published in 1978.

- John Banville's 1997 novel *The Untouchable* is a fictionalized biography of Blunt that includes a character based on Philby.

- Philby was the inspiration for the character of British intelligence officer Archibald "Arch" Cummings in the 2006 film *The Good Shepherd*. Cummings is played by Billy Crudup.

- The 2005 film *A Different Loyalty* is an unattributed account taken from Eleanor Philby's book, *Kim Philby: The Spy I Loved*. The film recounts Philby's love affair and marriage to Eleanor Brewer during his time in Beirut and his eventual defection to the Soviet Union in late January 1963, though the characters based on Philby and Brewer have different names.

In music

- In the song "Philby", from the *Top Priority* album (1979), Rory Gallagher draws parallels between his life on the road and a spy's in a foreign country. Sample lyrics : "Now ain't it strange that I feel like Philby / There's a stranger in my soul / I'm lost in transit in a lonesome city / I can't come in from the cold".

- The Philby affair is mentioned in the Simple Minds song "Up on the Catwalk" from their sixth studio album *Sparkle in the Rain*. The lyrics are: "Up on the catwalk, and you dress in waistcoats / And got brillantino, and friends of Kim Philby".

- The song "Angleton", by Russian indie rock band Biting Elbows, focuses largely on Philby's role as a spy from the perspective of James Jesus Angleton.

- The song 'Traitor' by Renegade Soundwave from their album *Soundclash* mentions "Philby, Burgess and Maclean" with the lyrics "snitch, grass, informer, you're a traitor; you can't be trusted and left alone".

- The song "Kim Philby", from the self-titled album by Vancouver punk band Terror of Tiny Town (1994) includes the line, "They say he was the third man, but he's number one with us." The lead singer and accordionist of the now defunct band was political satirist Geoff Berner.

Other

- The 1993 Joseph Brodsky essay *Collector's Item* (published in his 1995 book *On Grief and Reason*) contains a conjectured description of Philby's career, as well as speculations into his motivations and general thoughts on espionage and politics. The title of the essay refers to a postal stamp commemorating Philby issued in the Soviet Union in the late 1980s.

Further reading

- Colonel David Smiley, "Irregular Regular", Michael Russell – Norwich – 1994 (ISBN 978-0-85955-202-8). Translated in French by Thierry Le Breton, Au coeur de l'action clandestine des commandos au MI6, L'Esprit du Livre Editions, France, 2008 (ISBN 978-2-915960-27-3). With numerous photographs. Memoirs of a SOE and MI6 officer during the Valuable Project.

- Genrikh Borovik, *The Philby Files*, 1994, published by Little, Brown & Company Limited, Canada, ISBN 0-316-91015-5 . Introduction by Phillip Knightley.

- Phillip Knightley, *Philby: KGB Masterspy* 2003, published by Andre Deutsch Ltd, London, ISBN 978-0-233-00048-0. 1st American edition has title: *The Master Spy: the Story of Kim Philby*, ISBN 0394578902

- Phillip Knightley, *The Second Oldest Profession: Spies and Spying in the Twentieth Century*, 1986, published by W.W. Norton & Company, London.

- Kim Philby, *My Silent War*, published by Macgibbon & Kee Ltd, London, 1968, or Granada Publishing, ISBN 978-0-586-02860-5. Introduction by Graham Greene, well known author who worked with and for Philby in British intelligence services.

- Bruce Page, David Leitch and Phillip Knightley, *Philby: The Spy Who Betrayed a Generation*, 1968, published by André Deutsch, Ltd., London.

- Michael Smith, *The Spying Game*, 2003, published by Politico's, London.

- Richard Beeston, *Looking For Trouble: The Life and Times of a Foreign Correspondent*, 1997, published by Brassey's, London.

- Desmond Bristow, *A Game of Moles*, 1993, published by Little Brown & Company, London.

- Miranda Carter, *Anthony Blunt: His Lives*, 2001, published by Farrar, Straus and Giroux, New York.

- Anthony Cave Brown, *"C": The Secret Life of Sir Stewart Graham Menzies, Spymaster to Winston Churchill*, 1987, published by Macmillan, New York.

- John Fisher, *Burgess and Maclean*, 1977, published by Robert Hale, London.

- S. J. Hamrick, *Deceiving the Deceivers*, 2004, published by Yale University Press, New Haven.

- Malcolm Muggeridge, *The Infernal Grove: Chronicles of Wasted Time: Number 2*, 1974, published by William Morrow & Company, New York.

- Barrie Penrose & Simon Freeman, *Conspiracy of Silence: The Secret Life of Anthony Blunt*, 1986, published by Farrar Straus Giroux, New York.

- Anthony Cave Brown, 'Treason in the Blood: H. St. John Philby, Kim Philby, and the Spy Case of the Century, *Boston, Houghton Mifflin, 1994, ISBN 0-395-63119-X.*

- Richard C.S. Trahair and Robert Miller, *Encyclopedia of Cold War Espionage, Spies, and Secret Operations*, 2009, published by Enigma Books, New York. ISBN 978-1-929631-75-9

- Nigel West, editor, *The Guy Liddell Diaries: Vol. I: 1939–1942*, 2005, published by Routledge, London

- Nigel West & Oleg Tsarev, *The Crown Jewels: The British Secrets at the Heart of the KGB Archives*, 1998, published by Yale University Press, New Haven.

- Bill Bristow, "My Father The Spy" Deceptions of an MI6 Officer. Published by WBML Publishers. 2012.

- Desmond Bristow. With Bill Bristow. *"A Game of Moles" The Deceptions of and MI6 Officer*. Published 1993 by Little Brown and Warner.

The author acknowledges and wishes to thank Wikipedia and the Wikimedia Foundation for their invaluable inputs to this Biography.

James Jesus Angleton

James Jesus Angleton (December 9, 1917 – May 11, 1987) was chief of counterintelligence for the Central Intelligence Agency (CIA) from 1954 to 1974. His official position within the organization was Associate Deputy Director of Operations for Counterintelligence (ADDOCI). Angleton was significantly involved in the US response to the purported KGB defectors Anatoliy Golitsyn and Yuri Nosenko. Angleton later became convinced the CIA harbored a high-ranking mole, and engaged in an intensive search. Whether this was a highly destructive witch hunt or appropriate caution vindicated by later moles remains a subject of intense historical debate.

According to Director of Central Intelligence Richard Helms: "In his day, Jim was recognized as the dominant counterintelligence figure in the non-communist world." Investigative journalist Edward Jay Epstein agrees with the high regard in which Angleton was held by his colleagues in the intelligence business, and adds that Angleton earned the "trust...of six CIA directors—including Gen. Walter Bedell Smith, Allen W. Dulles and Richard Helms. They kept Angleton in key positions and valued his work."

Early and personal life

James Jesus Angleton was born in Boise, Idaho, to James Hugh Angleton and Carmen Mercedes Moreno. His parents met in Arizona while his father was a U.S. Army cavalry officer serving under General John Pershing. His father then joined the National Cash Register Corporation, rising through its ranks until in the early 1930s he purchased the NCR franchise in Italy, where he became head of the American Chamber of Commerce.

Angleton's boyhood was spent in Milan, Italy, where his family moved after his father bought NCR's Italian subsidiary. He then studied as a boarder at Malvern College in England before attending Yale University. The young Angleton was a poet and, as a Yale undergraduate, editor, with Reed Whittemore, of the Yale literary magazine *Furioso*, which published many of the best-known poets of the inter-war period, including William Carlos Williams, E. E. Cummings and Ezra Pound. He carried on an extensive correspondence with Pound, Cummings and T. S. Eliot, among others, and was particularly influenced by William Empson, author of *Seven Types of Ambiguity*. Angleton was trained in the New Criticism at Yale by Maynard Mack and others, chiefly Norman Holmes Pearson, a founder of American Studies, and briefly studied law at Harvard, but did not graduate.

He joined the U.S. Army in March 1943 and in July 1943 married Cicely Harriet d'Autremont, a Vassar alumna from Tucson, Arizona. Together, they had three children: James C. Angleton, Esq., Guru Sangat Kaur Khalsa (formerly Truffy Angleton, and Siri Hari Kaur Angleton-Khalsa (formerly Lucy d'Autremont Angleton). They lived in the Rock Spring neighborhood of Arlington, Virginia until Angleton's death in 1987. Angleton's wife and his daughters explored Sikhism. Both of Angleton's daughters became followers of Harbhajan Singh Khalsa.

A heavy drinker, towards the end of his life James Angleton was consuming 150-200 units of alcohol a week.

World War Two

During World War II Angleton served in the Office of Strategic Services (OSS) and led its branch in Italy.[1] He served under Norman Holmes Pearson in the counter-intelligence branch (X-2) of the Office of Strategic Services in London, where he met the famous double agent Kim Philby. Angleton was chief of the Italy desk for X-2 in London by February 1944 and in November was transferred to Italy as commander of SCI [Secret Counterintelligence] Unit Z, which handled Ultra intelligence based on the British intercepts of German radio communications.

By the end of the war, he was head of X-2 for all of Italy. In this position Angleton helped Junio Valerio Borghese, whose elite unit Decima MAS had collaborated with the SS, escape execution. Angleton was interested in the defense of installations such as ports and bridges and offered Borghese a fair trial, in return for his collaboration.[15] He dressed him up in an American uniform and drove him from Milan to Rome for interrogation by the Allies. Borghese was then tried and convicted of collaboration with the Nazi invaders but not of war crimes, by the Italian court.

Angleton remained in Italy after the war, establishing connections with other secret intelligence services and playing a major role in the victory of the US-supported Christian Democratic Party, over the USSR-supported Italian Communist Party in the 1948 elections.

CIA Career

Rise in influence in the CIA

Returning to Washington, he was employed by the various successor organizations to the OSS, eventually becoming one of the founder-officers of the Central Intelligence Agency in 1947. In May 1949, he was made head of Staff A of the CIA's Office of Special Operations, where he was responsible for the collection of foreign intelligence and liaison with the CIA's counterpart organizations. Beginning in 1951, Angleton was responsible for liaison with Israel's Mossad and Shin Bet agencies, "the Israeli desk", crucial relationships that he managed for the remainder of his career. During the next five years, Angleton helped put in place the structure of the new Agency and participated, to some extent, in the "Rollback" operations, associated with Frank Wisner in Albania, Poland and other countries, concerning all of which Angleton counseled caution and all of which failed. He worked particularly closely with Kim Philby, who being groomed to head the Secret Intelligence Service MI6, was also in Washington. The Angletons developed a varied social set in Washington, including professional acquaintances like the Philbys, poets, painters and journalists. In 1951, Philby's colleagues Guy Burgess and Donald Maclean defected to Moscow. Philby was expelled from Washington, suspected of having tipped them off to imminent exposure based on decoded Soviet communications from the Venona project.

Chief of the counterintelligence staff of the CIA

In 1954 Allen Dulles, who had recently become Director of Central Intelligence, named Angleton chief of the Counterintelligence Staff, a position that Angleton retained for the rest of his CIA career. Dulles also assigned Angleton responsibility for coordination with allied intelligence services. In general, Angleton's career at the CIA can be divided into three areas of responsibility: foreign intelligence activities, counterintelligence and domestic intelligence activities.

Under the heading of foreign intelligence, there was the Israeli desk, the "Lovestone Empire" and a variety of smaller operations. The Israeli connection was at first of interest to Angleton, for the information that could be obtained about the Soviet Union and aligned countries, from émigrés to Israel from those countries and for the utility of the Israeli foreign intelligence units, for proxy operations in third countries. Angleton's connections with the Israeli secret intelligence services were useful, for example, in obtaining from the Israeli Shin Bet a transcript of Nikita Khrushchev's 1956 speech to the Communist Party of the Soviet Union Congress denouncing Joseph Stalin. The *Lovestone Empire* is a term for the network run for the CIA by Jay Lovestone, once head of the Communist Party of the United States, later a trade union leader, who worked with foreign unions, using covert funds to construct a worldwide system of anti-communist unions. Finally, there were individual agents, especially in Italy, who reported to Angleton. [17] It is quite possible that there were other foreign intelligence activities for which Angleton was responsible, for example, in Southeast Asia and in the Caribbean.

Angleton's primary responsibilities as chief of the counterintelligence staff of the CIA have given rise to a considerable literature focused on his efforts to identify any Soviet or Eastern Bloc agents, working in American secret intelligence agencies. As such agents have come to be called "moles", operations intended to find them have come to be called "Molehunts".

Three books dealing with Angleton take these matters as their central theme: Tom Mangold's Cold Warrior: James Jesus Angleton: The CIA's Master Spy Hunter, David C. Martin's Wilderness of Mirrors: Intrigue, Deception, and the Secrets that Destroyed Two of the Cold War's Most Important Agents and David Wise's Molehunt: The Secret Search for Traitors that Shattered the CIA. Tim Weiner's Legacy of Ashes: The History of the CIA paints Angleton as an incompetent alcoholic. These views have been challenged by Mark Riebling in Wedge: The Secret War between the FBI and CIA.

Angleton thought that all secret intelligence agencies should be assumed to be penetrated by others, or, at least, that a reasonable chief of counterintelligence should assume so. Angleton had direct experience of ways in which secret intelligence services could be penetrated. There was the manipulation of the German services in World War II by means of Ultra; there was the direct penetration of the British services by the Cambridge Five and their indirect penetration of the American services by means of the liaison activities of Kim Philby, Donald Maclean and perhaps others, and there were the highly successful efforts of the American secret intelligence services in regard to allied, hostile and Third World services. The combination of Angleton's close association with Philby and Philby's duplicity caused Angleton to double-check "potential problems". Philby was confirmed as a Soviet mole, when he eluded those sent to capture him and defected. Philby said that Angleton had been "a brilliant opponent" and a fascinating friend who seemed to be "catching on" before Philby's departure, thanks to CIA employee William King Harvey, a former Federal Bureau of Investigation agent, who had voiced his suspicions regarding Philby and others, who Angleton suspected were Soviet agents.

Angleton's position in the CIA, his close relationship with Richard Helms, in particular, his experience and character, made him particularly influential. As in all bureaucracies, this influence brought him the enmity of those who had different views. The conflict between the "Angletonians" and the "Anti-Angletonians" has played out in the public sphere generally in publications about the mole hunts and, in particular, in regard to two Soviet defectors (among many): Anatoliy Golitsyn and Yuri Nosenko.

Golitsyn and Nosenko

Although Golitsyn was a questionable source, Angleton accepted significant information obtained from his debriefing by the CIA. It is claimed that Golitsyn, in asking to defect rather than to become a double agent, implied that the CIA had already been seriously compromised by the KGB. Golitsyn may have concluded that the CIA failed to debrief him correctly because his debriefing was misdirected by a mole in the Soviet Russia Division, limiting his debriefing to a review of photographs of Soviet embassy staff to identify KGB officers and refusing to discuss KGB strategy. After Golitsyn raised this possibility with MI5 in a subsequent debriefing in Britain, MI5 raised the same concern with Angleton, who responded by requesting that DCI Richard Helms allow him to assume responsibility for Golitsyn and his further debriefing.

In 1964, Yuri Nosenko, a KGB officer working out of Geneva, Switzerland, insisted that he needed to defect to the US, as his role as a double agent had been discovered, prompting his recall to Moscow. Nosenko was allowed to defect, although his credibility was immediately in question because the CIA was unable to verify a KGB recall order. Nosenko made two controversial claims: that Golitsyn was not a defector but a KGB plant, and that he had information on the assassination of President John F. Kennedy by way of the KGB's history with Lee Harvey Oswald during the time that Oswald lived in the Soviet Union.

Regarding the first claim, Golitsyn had said from the beginning that the KGB would try to plant other defectors in an effort to discredit him. Regarding the second, Nosenko told his debriefers that he had been personally responsible for handling Oswald's case and that the KGB had judged Oswald unfit for service due to his mental instability. Nosenko claimed that the KGB had not even attempted to debrief Oswald about his work on the U-2 spy plane during his service in the United States Marine Corps. Although other KGB sources corroborated Nosenko's story, he repeatedly failed lie detector tests. Judging the claim of not interrogating Oswald about the U-2 improbable, given Oswald's familiarity with the U-2 program, and faced with further challenges to Nosenko's credibility (he also falsely claimed to be a lieutenant colonel, a higher rank than he in fact held), Angleton did not object when David Murphy, then head of the Soviet Russia Division, ordered Nosenko held in solitary confinement for approximately three-and-a-half years.

Contrary to some accounts, the detention of Nosenko was neither ordered by Angleton nor kept secret. Without naming Nosenko, the 1975 report of the Rockefeller Commission, also known as the President's Commission on CIA Activities within the United States, affirmed that the CIA's Office of Security, which is responsible for the safety of defectors, the Attorney General, the Federal Bureau of Investigation (FBI), the United States Intelligence Board, and select members of Congress were all apprised of Nosenko's detention. Nosenko never changed his story. The "Monster Plot" report about Nosenko's detainment and handling, written by John Hart, was feared by him and CIA lawyers to be libelous due to including "literally irrelevant" information and "dramatic rhetorical phrases."

Suspicion of infiltration

Angleton became increasingly convinced that the CIA was compromised by the KGB.[21] Golitsyn convinced him that the KGB had reorganized in 1958 and 1959 to consist mostly of a shell, incorporating only those agents whom the CIA and the FBI were recruiting, directed by a small cabal of puppet masters who doubled those agents to manipulate their Western counterparts. Hoover eventually curbed cooperation with the CIA, because Angleton refused to relent on this hypothesis. Angleton also came into increasing conflict with the rest of the CIA, particularly with the Directorate of Operations, over the efficacy of their intelligence-gathering efforts, which he questioned without explaining his broader views on KGB strategy and organization. DCI Helms was not willing to tolerate the resulting paralysis. Golitsyn, who was after all a major in the KGB and had defected years before, was

144

able to marshal few facts to provide concrete support for his far-reaching theoretical views of the KGB. The senior leadership of the CIA came to this conclusion after a hearing in 1968 and Angleton was thereafter unable to draw directly upon Golitsyn.

In the period of the Vietnam War and Soviet-American détente, Angleton was convinced of the necessity of the war and believed that the strategic calculations underlying the resumption of relations with China were based on a deceptive KGB staging of the Sino-Soviet split. He went so far as to speculate that Henry Kissinger might be under KGB influence. During this period, Angleton's counter-intelligence staff undertook a most comprehensive domestic covert surveillance project (called Operation CHAOS) under the direction of President Lyndon Johnson. The prevailing belief at the time was that the anti-war and civil rights movements of the 1960s and 1970s had foreign funding and support. None was found by them, although the Soviet Union did influence the movements (see Soviet influence on the peace movement).

DCI William Colby reorganized the CIA in an effort to curb Angleton's influence, beginning by stripping him of control over the Israeli "account", which had the effect of weakening counter-intelligence. Colby then demanded Angleton's resignation. It has been claimed that Angleton directed CIA assistance to the Israeli nuclear weapons program.[23]

Throughout the 1960s and 1970s Angleton privately accused various foreign leaders of being Soviet spies. He twice informed the Royal Canadian Mounted Police that he believed Prime Minister Lester Pearson and his successor Pierre Trudeau were agents of the Soviet Union. In 1964, under pressure from Angleton, the RCMP detained John Watkins, a close friend of Pearson and formerly Canadian Ambassador to the Soviet Union. Watkins died during interrogation by the RCMP and was subsequently cleared of suspicion. Angleton accused Swedish Prime Minister Olof Palme, West German Chancellor Willy Brandt and British Prime Minister Harold Wilson of using their access to NATO secrets to benefit the USSR.

Attempted removal of Gough Whitlam

Australian journalist Brian Toohey claimed that Angleton considered then Australian Prime Minister Gough Whitlam a "serious threat" to the US and was concerned after the Commonwealth police raided ASIO headquarters in Melbourne in 1973 at the direction of Attorney General Lionel Murphy. In 1974, Angleton sought to instigate the removal of Whitlam from office by having CIA station chief in Canberra, John Walker, ask Peter Barbour, then head of ASIO, to make a false declaration that Whitlam had lied about the raid in Parliament. Barbour refused to make the statement.

Resignation

Seymour Hersh published a story in *The New York Times* about domestic counter-intelligence activities under Angleton's direction, against anti-war protesters and other domestic dissident organizations. Following this, Angleton's resignation was announced on Christmas Eve of 1974, just as President Gerald Ford demanded that Colby report on the allegations and as various Congressional committees announced that they would launch their own inquiries. Angleton told reporters from United Press International that he was quitting after 31 years because "my usefulness has ended" and the CIA was getting involved in "police state activities." Three of Angleton's senior aides in counter-intelligence—his deputy Raymond Rocca, executive officer of the counter-intelligence division William J. Hood, and Angleton's chief of operations Newton S. Miller—were coaxed into retirement within a week of Angleton's resignation after it was made clear that they would be transferred elsewhere in the agency rather than promoted, and the counter-intelligence staff was reduced from 300 to 80 people. In 1975, Angleton was awarded the CIA's Distinguished Intelligence Medal.[26] By this time, Angleton had been quietly rehired by the CIA at his old salary through a secret contract. Until September 1975, "operational issues remained solely the preserve of Angleton."

Death

Angleton died from cancer in Washington D.C. on 11 May 1987.

Legacy

Angleton's tour of duty in Italy as an intelligence officer is regarded as a critical turn not only in his professional life, wherein he helped recover Nazi looted treasures from other European countries and Africa, but also for the Agency. Angleton's personal liaisons with Italian Mafia figures helped the CIA in the immediate period after World War II. Angleton took charge of the CIA's effort to subvert Italian elections, to prevent communist and communist-related parties from gaining political leverage in the parliament.

Deception is a state of mind—and the mind of the state.

In time, Angleton's zeal and suspicions came to be regarded as counter-productive, if not destructive, for the CIA. In the wake of his departure, counter-intelligence efforts were undertaken with far less enthusiasm. Some believe this overcompensation was responsible for oversights which allowed Aldrich Ames, Robert Hanssen and many others to compromise the CIA, the FBI and other agencies long after Angleton's resignation. Although the American intelligence community quickly bounced back from the embarrassments of the Church Committee, it found itself uncharacteristically incapable of policing itself after Angleton's departure.

Edward Jay Epstein is among those who have argued that the positions of Ames and Hanssen—both well-placed Soviet counter-intelligence agents, in the CIA and FBI respectively—would enable the KGB to deceive the American intelligence community, in the manner that Angleton hypothesized.

The 1970s were generally a period of upheaval for the CIA. During George H. W. Bush's tenure as DCI, President Ford authorized the creation of a "Team B" under the aegis of the President's Foreign Intelligence Advisory Board. This project concluded that the Agency and the intelligence community had seriously underestimated Soviet strategic nuclear strength in Central Europe in their National Intelligence Estimate. The Church Commission brought no small number of skeletons out of the Agency's closet. The organization inherited by Admiral Stansfield Turner on his appointment as DCI by President Jimmy Carter in 1977, was shortly to face further cuts, and Turner used Angleton as an example of the excesses in the Agency that he hoped to curb, both during his service and in his memoirs.

The suspicions of Angleton and his staff impeded the career advancement of a number of CIA employees. The CIA later paid out compensation to three, under what Agency employees termed the "Mole Relief Act". Forty employees are said to have been investigated and fourteen considered serious suspects by Angleton's staff.

When Golitsyn defected, he claimed that the CIA had a mole who had been stationed in West Germany, was of Slavic descent, had a last name that might end in "sky" and definitely began with a "K", and operated under the KGB codename "Sasha". Angleton believed this claim, with the result that anyone who approximated this description fell under his suspicion. Some within CIA considered Golitsyn discredited even before Angleton's ousting, but the two did not appear to have lost their faith in one another. They sought the assistance of William F. Buckley, Jr. (himself once in the CIA) in authoring *New Lies for Old*, which advanced the argument that the USSR planned to fake its collapse to lull its enemies into a false sense of victory, but Buckley refused. In his book *Wedge: The Secret War between the FBI and CIA* (Knopf, 1994), Mark Riebling stated that of 194 predictions made in *New Lies For Old*, 139 had been fulfilled by 1993, nine seemed 'clearly wrong', and the other 46 were 'not soon falsifiable'.

Despite misgivings over his uncompromising and often obsessive approach to his profession, Angleton is highly regarded by a number of his peers in the intelligence business. Former Shin Bet chief Amos Manor, in an interview in *Ha'aretz*, revealed his fascination for the man during Angleton's work to forge the U.S.–Israel liaison in the early 1950s. Manor described Angleton as "fanatic about everything", with a "tendency towards mystification". Manor discovered decades later that the real reason for Angleton's visit to him was to investigate Manor, being an Eastern European Jewish immigrant, for James Angleton thought that it would be prudent to "sanitize" the U.S.–Israeli bridge before a more formal intelligence relationship was established.

CIA Family Jewels

Main article: Family Jewels (Central Intelligence Agency)

A set of highly sensitive Agency documents, referred to as the "Family Jewels," was publicly released on June 25, 2007, after more than three decades of secrecy.[31][32] The release was prompted by an internal CIA investigation of the 1970s Church Committee which verified the far-ranging power and influence that Angleton wielded during his long tenure as counterintelligence czar. The exposé revealed that Angleton-planned infiltration of law enforcement and military organizations in other countries was used to increase the influence of the United States. It also confirmed past rumors that it was Angleton who was in charge of the domestic spying activities of the CIA under Operation CHAOS.

In popular culture

- The 2006 film *The Good Shepherd* is loosely based on Angleton's life and his role in the formation of the CIA.[34]

- *The Laundry Files* by Charles Stross features a senior Laundry agent whose *nom de guerre* is James Angleton after the CIA chief.[35]

- The 2007 television mini-series *The Company* focus on Angleton's efforts to find a Soviet mole. Angleton was portrayed by Michael Keaton.

- Angleton was portrayed by John Light in the 2003 BBC TV mini-series *Cambridge Spies*.

- The song "Angleton" by Russian indie rock band Biting Elbows is about Angleton's life and career.[36]

- In the television series *Granite Flats* the actor Cary Elwes plays Hugh Ashmead, the name "Ashmead" being the cover name for James J. Angleton.

- William F. Buckley's 2000 novel *Spytime: The Undoing of James Jesus Angleton* is a fictionalized treatment of Angleton's career, a storyline being placed upon, between and within actual historic facts and events.[37]

- Mike Doughty released a song entitled "James Jesus Angleton" on Apple Music in December 2017.[38]

- The Fatima Mansions track "Brunceling's song" mentions James Jesus Angleton by name, in a narrative involving spooks adapting to regular life.

- In the 1991 novel Harlot's Ghost, Tremont Montague (Harlot) is based on Angleton.[39]

- The fourth season of the television series Le Bureau des Légendes introduces a character from the French external security service (DGSE) with the nickname of "JJA" - James Jesus Angleton. There is a short discussion of Angleton's career and its connection to this character.

The author acknowledges and wishes to thank Wikipedia and the Wikimedia Foundation for their invaluable inputs to this Biography.

ABOUT THE AUTHOR

Dr. Anthony R. Wells (taken in Prague, Czech Republic)

Anthony Wells is unique insofar as he is the only living person to have worked for British intelligence as a British citizen and US intelligence as a US citizen, and to have also served in uniform at sea and ashore with both the Royal Navy and the US Navy. He is a fifty-year veteran of the Five Eyes intelligence community. In 2017 he was the keynote speaker on board HMS *Victory* in Portsmouth, England, to commemorate the hundredth anniversary of the famous Zimmermann Telegram intelligence coup by "Blinker" Hall and his Room 40 team in British Naval Intelligence. The guest of honor was Her Royal Highness Princess Anne, with the Five Eyes community, past and present, representing the United States, the United Kingdom, Canada, Australia, and New Zealand in attendance. Dr. Wells, or Commander Wells, was trained and mentored in the late 1960s by the very best of the World War Two intelligence community, including Sir Harry Hinsley, the famous

Bletchley Park code breaker, official historian of British intelligence in the Second World War, master of St. John's College, Cambridge, and vice chancellor of Cambridge University. Sir Harry Hinsley introduced Dr. Wells to the Enigma data before it became public knowledge. Dr. Wells received his PhD in war studies from King's College, University of London, in 1972. He holds bachelor's and master's degrees from the University of Durham, and a master's degree from the London School of Economics. He was trained at Britannia Royal Naval College, Dartmouth, and received his advanced training at the School of Maritime Operations. He was called to the bar by Lincoln's Inn in November 1980. Anthony Wells has four children and eight grandchildren and lives on his farm in Virginia. He is a member of the Naval Order of the United States and was appointed an Honorary Crew Member of USS *Liberty* by the USS *Liberty* Veterans Association. USS *Liberty* is the most highly decorated warship in the history of the US Navy for a single action: when it was attacked by Israeli air and surface forces on August 8, 1967, in the eastern Mediterranean. Dr. Wells is the third chairman of the USS *Liberty* Alliance, succeeding the later Admiral Thomas Moorer, former chairman of the US Joint Chiefs of Staff and chief of Naval Operations; and the late Rear Admiral Clarence "Mark" Hill, former distinguished US naval aviator and battle group commander. He is a retired US National Ski Patrol patroller and instructor and a life member and former president of The Plains, Virginia, Volunteer Fire Rescue Company. Wells is an FAA commercial pilot with single and multiengine, land and sea, instrument, and flight instructor ratings.

ANTHONY WELLS'S PUBLICATIONS

Literary Awards: In 2013 and 2017, the United States Naval Submarine League presented Dr. Anthony R. Wells with Literary Awards for Articles in *The Submarine Review.*

Books

German Public Opinion and Hitler's Policies, 1933-39. 1968. Electronic version available at Durham University Library, UK—access Durham University Library website and search database using title and/or author name. Electronic and hard copy versions available.

Studies in British Naval Intelligence, 1880-1945. 1972. Electronic version available online via the British Library (ETHOS) and also King's College, London—visit either site and search the database using title and/or author name. Electronic and hard copy versions available.

Training and the Achievement of Management Objectives, the Solution of Management Problems, and as an Instrument of Organizational Change. 1974. The London School of Economics and Political Science.

Technical Change and British Naval Policy. Edited by Bryan Ranft. Hodder and Stoughton, London, 1977; and Holmes and Meier, New York, NY.

War and Society. Edited by Brian Bond and Ian Roy. Croom Helm, London, 1977; and Holmes and Meier, New York, NY.

Soviet Naval Diplomacy. Edited by B. Dismukes and J. McConnell. Pergamon Press, 1979.

The Soviet and Other Communist Navies. Edited by James George. US Naval Institute Press, Annapolis, Maryland, 1986.

Black Gold Finale. Dorrance Publishing Company, 2009.

The Golden Few. Dorrance Publishing Company, 2012.

A Tale of Two Navies: Geopolitics, Technology, and Strategy in the United States and the Royal Navy, 1960-2015. US Naval Institute Press, Annapolis, Maryland, January 2017.

Between Five Eyes. Casemate Publishers, Oxford, UK; and Havertown, PA, September 2020.

Room39 and the Lisbon Connection. Xlibris, Bloomington, Indiana, June 2021.

Crossroads in Time: Philby & Angleton—A Story of Treachery. Palmetto Publishing, North Charleston, South Carolina. A novel. December 2021.

Articles

Admirals Hall and Godfrey—Doyens of Naval Intelligence (Two Parts). The Naval Review, 1973.

Staff Training and the Royal Navy (Two Parts). The Naval Review, 1975, 1976.

The 1967 June War: Soviet Naval Diplomacy and the Sixth Fleet—A Reappraisal. Center for Naval Analyses, Arlington, Virginia. Professional Paper 204, October 1977.

The Center for Naval Analyses. Professional Paper Number 197, December 1977. Department of the Navy, Washington, DC, Center for Naval Analyses.

The Soviet Navy in the Arctic and North Atlantic. National Defense, February 1986.

Soviet Submarine Prospects 1985-2000. Submarine Review, January 1986.

A New Defense Strategy for Britain. Proceedings of the United States Naval Institute, March 1987.

Presence and Military Strategies of the USSR in the Arctic. Quebec Center for International Relations, Laval University, 1986.

Real Time Targeting: Myth or Reality. Proceedings of the United States Naval Institute, August 2001.

Missing Magics Machine Material. New Insights on December 7, 1941 and Relevance for Today's Navy. The Submarine Review, April 2003.

US Naval Power and the Pursuit of Peace in an Era of International Terrorism and Weapons of Mass Destruction. The Submarine Review, October 2002.

Transformation—Some Insights and Observations for the Royal Navy from across the Atlantic. The Naval Review, August 2003.

They Did Not Die in Vain. USS Liberty Incident—Some Additional Perspectives. Proceedings of the United States Naval Institute, March 2005.

Royal Navy at the Crossroads: Turn the Strategic Tide. A Way to Implement a Lasting Vision. The Naval Review, November 2010.

The Royal Navy Is Key to Britain's Security Strategy. Proceedings of the United States Naval Institute, December 2010.

The Survivability of the Royal Navy and a New Enlightened British Defense Strategy. The Submarine Review, January 2011.

A Strategy in East Asia that Can Endure. Proceedings of the United States Naval Institute, May 2011.

A Strategy in East Asia that Can Endure. The Naval Review, August 2011. Reprinted by kind permission of the United States Naval Institute.

The United States Navy, Jordan, and a Long Term Israeli-Palestinian Security Agreement. The Submarine Review, Spring 2012

Admiral Sir Herbert Richmond: What Would He Think, Write and Action today? The Naval Review, February 2013—Lead article in the Centenary Edition of The Naval Review.

Postscript to Missing Magics Machine Material—Tribute to a Great Submariner: Captain Edward Beach, US Navy. The Submarine Review, 2013.

Jordan, Israel, and US Need to Cooperate for Missile Defense. USNI News, March 26, 2103.

A Tribute to Admiral Sir John "Sandy" Woodward. USNI News, August 8, 2013

USS Liberty Document Center. Edited by Anthony Wells and Thomas Schaaf. A website produced by SiteWhirks, Inc., Warrenton, Virginia. September 2013. In April 2017 this website was transferred to the Library of Congress for permanent safekeeping for the use of future scholars and researchers.

The Future of ISIS: A Joint US-Russian Assessment. With Dr. Andrey Chuprygin. The Naval Review, May 2015.

The Zimmermann Telegram: 100th Anniversary. The Naval Review, February 2017; and The Submarine Review, 2017.

Put The Guns in a Box. With Captain J. W. Phillips, US Navy retired. Proceedings of the US Naval Institute, June 2018.

Quo Vadis China? A View from Across the Atlantic, Part 1. The Naval Review, November 2019.

Quo Vadis China? The Submarine Review, December 2019.

USS Amberjack and the Attack on USS Liberty. With Mr. Larry Taylor, ST1 USS Amberjack. US Naval Institute Naval History Blog, January 7, 2020.

USS Amberjack and the Attack on USS Liberty. With Mr. Larry Taylor. The Submarine Review, March 2020.

The UK's Strategic Defense and Security Review, A US Perspective. The Submarine Review, June 2020.

The United Kingdom Needs a Maritime Strategy. The Naval Review, August 2020.

Submarines and the Ring of Fire in the Indo Pacific Theater: A Strategic Analysis. The Submarine Review, December 2020.

UK's Defense & Security Review—Some Final Observations. The Naval Review, Autumn 2020.

A Brave New World of Next Generation Technologies. Warship World: Volume 17, Number 2, January/February 2021.

To Honor the Last Nuremburg Prosecutor. Proceedings of the United States Naval Institute, Annapolis, Maryland, May 2021.

The United Nations Convention on the Law of the Sea and the United States Navy. US Naval Institute Blog, June 2021.

Is There a Need for a New Generation of Submarine Officers Who Are
     Intelligence Trained and Experienced beyond Current Levels? And
     How Might We Learn from the Past? The Submarine Review, June
     2021.
Behind the Five Eyes. Counsel Magazine (Justice Matters: Spotlight section),
     the monthly magazine of the Bar of England & Wales, London, UK,
     July 2021.
Letter from The Plains. A monthly article in the Middleburg Eccentric,
     Virginia, since 2016.

Reports
NATO and US Carrier Deployment Policies. Center for Naval Analyses,
     Arlington, Virginia, February 1977.
NATO and US Carrier Deployment Policies, Formation of a New Standing
     Naval Strike Force in NATO. Center for Naval Analyses, Arlington,
     Virginia, April 1977.
Sea War '85 Scenario. With Captain John L. Underwood, USN. Center for
     Naval Analyses, Arlington, Virginia, June 1977.
Submarine Construction Program for the State of Sabah, Malaysia. RDA
     Contract TR-188600-OOl, December 1984. Chief Minister of Sabah,
     Malaysia, and Government of Malaysia.
The Application of Drag Reduction and Boundary Layer Control Technologies
     in an Experimental Program. For the Chief Naval Architect, Vickers
     Shipbuilding and Engineering Ltd, Barrow-in-Furness, UK. January
     1985.
The Strategic Importance and Advantages of Labuan, Federal Malaysian
     Territory, as a Naval Base with Special Reference to Its Capabilities as
     the Royal Malaysian Navy Submarine Base. Chief Minister of Sabah,
     Malaysia, and Government of Malaysia. March 1985.
Preliminary Overview of Soviet Merchant Ships in Anti-SSBN Operations and
     Soviet Merchant Ships and Submarine Masking. (Department of the
     Navy Contract N00016-85-C-0204).

SSBN Port Egress and the Non-Commercial Activities of the Soviet Merchant Fleet: Concepts of Operation and War Orders for Current and Future Anti-SSBN Operations. (Department of the Navy Contract 136400).

Overview Study of the Maritime Aspects of the Nuclear Balance in the European Theater (Department of Energy Study for the European Conflict Analysis Project). October 1986.

Soviet Submarine Warfare Strategy Assessment and Future US Submarine and Anti-Submarine Warfare Technologies (Defense Advanced Research Projects Agency, March 1988). RDA Contract 146601).

Limited Objective Experiment ZERO, July 2000. The Naval Air Systems Command, US Navy, Department of Defense. 2002.

Operational Factors Associated with the Software Nuclear Safety Analysis for the UGM-109A Tomahawk Submarine-Launched Land Attack Cruise Missile Combat Control System Mark I. United States Navy and Logicon Inc., 1989.

Operation Bahrain. The Assistant Director of Central Intelligence, the Central Intelligence Agency. March 2003.

Distributed Data Analysis with Bayesian Networks: A Preliminary Study for Non-Proliferation of Radioactive Devices, December 2003 (with F. Dowla and G. Larson). The Lawrence Livermore National Laboratory, Livermore, California, December 2003.

Fiber Reinforced Pumice Protective Barriers—To Mitigate the Effects of Suicide and Truck Bombs. Final Report and Recommendations. United States Navy, Washington, DC. With Professor Vistasp Kharbari, Professor of Structural Engineering, University of California, San Diego. August 2006.

Weapon Target Centric Model: Preliminary Modules and Applications, in Two Volumes. United States Navy, Principal Executive Officer Submarines, Washington, DC, August 2007.

Tactical Decision Aid (TDA). Multi-intelligence capability for national, theater, and tactical intelligence in real time across geographic space and time. The National Intelligence Community, Washington, DC, May 2012.

Submarine Industrial Base Model. Key industrial base model for the US VIRGINIA Class nuclear powered attack submarine, Principal

Executive Officer Submarines, Washington Navy Yard, Washington, DC, October 2012.

Manuals

Astro-Navigation: A Programmed Course in 6 Volumes for Training UK and Commonwealth Naval Officers in the Use of Astronomical Navigation at Sea. Royal Navy, Ministry of Defence, UK, 1969.

The Battle of Trafalgar: A Programmed Course in One Volume in Naval Strategy and Tactics. Royal Navy, Ministry of Defence, UK, 1969.

The Double Cross System: A Programmed Course in One Volume for British, Foreign and Commonwealth Naval Officers Attending the Royal Naval Staff College, Greenwich, UK. Royal Navy, Ministry of Defence, UK, 1973.

Unclassified Titles for Technology and Operational Areas— Covering Classified Programs—and Publications—Generic Areas

Airborne Mine Clearance

Streak Tube Imaging LIDAR

Magic Lantern Program

Tritium Microsphere Technology

Classified Applications of the Naval Simulation System

Naval Surface Fire Support and the Extended Range Guided Munition (ERGM)

Nonacoustic Antisubmarine Warfare

Battlefield Awareness and Data Dissemination (BADD Program)

Joint Stars Program Special Applications

Naval Fires Network

Littoral Surveillance System

Fleet Battle Experiment Operations (Technical Director FBE Alpha and FBE Bravo) Third Fleet, US Pacific Fleet

Ocean Surveillance (Radar and Optics)

Multispectral Applications
Space-Based Sensors and Surveillance
Microwave Radiometry Applications
Detection, Locating, and Tracking
Clandestine Operations and Intelligence Collection Operations
Support to Special Forces
Special Submarine Operations
Tagging Tracking and Surveillance
Battlespace Shaping and Real-Time Targeting
Covert and Clandestine Operations against Weapons of Mass Destruction and Other Major Threats to US Security
Special Sensor Technology
Covert and Overt Operations Planning and Execution
Reports and MOUs for Commander-in-Chief and Secretary Level Actions
Airborne Infrared Measurement System
Stealth and Counter Stealth
Counterintelligence Operations
Tactical Exploitation System and Joint Fires Network
Asymmetric Warfare Initiative—2003
Hairy Buffalo Program
Tracking of the al Qai'da Terrorist Network and Operations
Tactical Decision Aid (TDA) for Submarine ISR operations
Advanced Cyberattack and Defense Technologies and Operations
Shrouded Lightning Special Program
Nonlinear Junction Radar and Adaptive Regenerative Controller Special Program
Special Program in Jordan
Special Program in Malaysia
Special Program in Bahrain
Special Program in Abu Dhabi
Special Program in Saudi Arabia
Special Program with Commander United States Pacific Fleet
Special Tests at the US Naval Air Station Patuxent River, Maryland, September 2012

LISAC Special Program
Applications of the Robust Laser Interferometry (RLI) System and Technology
Special Support to a Combined Cheltenham UK and Maryland US Group
Special Support for Indo-Pacific Operations

Classified Titles & Publications: During the years 1968–2018, Dr. Wells has been the author, lead author, or a key author of multiple highly classified code-word documents at the top secret SCI level in both the United Kingdom and the United States.

THE END